VINEGAR SUNDAY

VINEGAR SUNDAY

KANKANA BASU

INDIALOG PUBLICATIONS PVT. LTD.

Published in October 2004

Indialog Publications Pvt. Ltd.
O - 22, Lajpat Nagar II
New Delhi - 110024
Ph.: 91-11-29839936/29830504
Fax: 91-11-29835221
www.indialog.co.in

Printed at Chaman Offset Printers, Darya Ganj, New Delhi

ISBN 81-87981-72-5

To my father,
For imparting to me the love of the written word

CONTENTS

INTRODUCTION

As you charge across the busy wide main road in front of the Sacred Heart Church, scuttling between cars and taxis and diving past double-decker buses bearing down on you, on reaching the other side of the road you will notice a small rickety gate. Most pedestrians rushing past on urgent missions (as in the case of most metropolitan cities) barely notice it. But on opening the gate and taking a few steps forward you are likely to fall into a time warp. For nestled among the gnarled, old, dust-laden trees is an ancient three-storey building. It is dilapidated with age, has old-fashioned teakwood doorways, a dark narrow staircase and incense-sticks burning at every silent sepia landing. The residents are mainly Bengalis (except the Sharmas on the third floor) and have been living here for generations. The lives of each family entwine with those of the others. The oldest lot wears striped pyjamas and reads T. S. Eliot reclining in armchairs placed in verandahs dappled with the long shadows of memories. The youngest read Pokemon, Harry Potter and chew gum. The middle generation wears tops that miss the navel and do not read at all (having more exciting things to do). According to the postman who has been delivering letters for years, the house is halfway to the railway station from the postoffice, halfway to the fresh-fish market from the station (an important point for the Bengali residents) and the residents a bunch of near-lunatics. The postman having a slightly poetic bent of mind named Building Number 6, Block 'G' "Halfway House." And in a matter of a few years the nickname attained official status.

THE MISFIT

On the ground floor of Halfway House, combining two adjacent flats lived the brothers Guha. This Sunday afternoon, the Guhas were all assembled for their usual post lunch laze-argue-burp session. The afternoon was dark and windy with the smell of fresh wet earth indicating rain somewhere close. It was so dark that the lights had to be put on and they lit up the shabby drawing room with a cozy golden glow.

Khokon was home on his monthly visit from the medical college hostel. He lay draped around the divan like a thin bespectacled python, steadily demolishing a high pyramid of "nimkis" made specially for him by his Kakima. His uncles were busy with a heated discussion about the dismal state of Indian cricket. It was an argument doomed to end in a stalemate and within minutes the uncles would train their cold searchlights on him. And like a deer trapped in the mesh of their bifocal glances, he would turn deaf and mute with his IQ plummeting to sub-zero depths. Khokon was four when his father died. His uncles had stepped in neatly and swiftly, taking over his upbringing with single-minded zeal. A son born after four girls (his uncles had two daughters each), his privileged position in the joint family was unrivalled. The fattest pieces of fish came to him, the creamiest portion of the milk was poured into his glass and the speed of the fan adjusted minutely when he sat down to eat. He would be fed, groomed and put into a prestigious professional institution. On graduating as a doctor/engineer/architect/cost accountant he would repay the family for the fish and the milk. He would then paint afresh the old house (pieces of plaster fell into the tea at times), repair the flushes (one had to manually pour buckets of water) and salvage the stiff Guha pride (in imminent danger of disintegration with the retirement of the uncles). A lot was being invested in Khokon and the stakes were high.

From the time he was six, Khokon had an obsession with time. He liked to surround himself with clocks of every kind. He wore three watches one beside the other on his right wrist and set alarms by the hour. One of his favourite activities was to sit in an armchair on quiet dark afternoons, while the whole house slumbered, and listen to the old grandfather clock ticking away. Passed on from generation to generation, the pendulum swung gently, catching the glint of silver at every alternate oscillation. Khokon felt intoxicated to just sit and feel the moments ticking by. So must they have ticked at the dawn of the universe, he thought, so must they have ticked in the gray rainy era of the dinosaurs and so would they tick when man, a speck in the procession of evolution vanished without a trace. He sat with his strange, whimsical fancies, draped around the chair dreamily till the clinking of tea things in the kitchen proclaimed evening.

Very few people understood Khokon. The only two true friends that he had in his growing years were Sharma Dadi upstairs and his youngest aunt "Kakima." His mother had turned into a stone-faced stranger long back, waiting and watching with narrowed eyes for the day he would get his graduation degree. His Kakima was only seven years older than him and passionately fond of kite-flying, roller-skating and science fiction movies. She smuggled him into dark matinee movie halls for the Star Wars trilogy (movies and such other frivolous things were forbidden by the uncles). She taught him to fly candlelit lanterns in the dead of the night. She referred to her elder brother-in-law as Yoda in private (on account of his being short, bald and wizened) and was the only person who could get Khokon rolling with mirth. As Khokon got older, she watched with misgiving how Khokon's mother joined hands with the uncles in the matter of his career. Rekhadi, she shook her head sadly, had gone over to the Dark side. Sharma Dadi loved Khokon unconditionally. She pulled him into her sweat-smelling armpits every morning and hugged him tight. She filled his pockets with almonds, to build up those biceps, she said with a wink. She did not approve of Khokon's diet. Rekha Guha should be giving him more of almonds, lassi, butter and red kidney beans. All this mustard fish business was no good for a boy's brawns. The boy was an uncut diamond, bless his soul, absolutely unpolluted and transparent. Wahe guru! Now if he and her granddaughter Sweety....

Khokon was reed-thin, wore horn-rimmed glasses and nondescript clothes. No one, not even his worst enemy (and he had none) could accuse him of being fashionable. In his intense contemplation of the evolution of the cosmos, he had quite forgotten to dress up. His brain functioned best and almost exclusively in a supine position, having spent his entire childhood draped around sofas, daydreaming. But this was a secret known only to Kakima and Sharma Dadi.

Khokon sat on the balcony in the mornings watching the sunlight play on silvery dew-drenched cobwebs. There! There was a moronic fly buzzing giddily right into the web. He could watch the spider-and-fly drama for hours. The quiet cunning of the spiders as they watched and waited out of sight vaguely reminded him of traffic cops who emerged unexpectedly out of trees, corners and sheer concrete pavements to nab his Kakima for jumping lights (something she did very often). A sizzled-looking frog emerging groggily from its long underground hibernation made his heart beat quicker, as did a wheel-sized rainbow at touching distance at a picnic waterfall. From September 22nd to October 22nd, he ate his dinner early. He then trudged up to the terrace with a folding chair to watch shooting stars. His Kakima had gifted him with a jumbo-sized mosquito repellant for these exciting nocturnal excursions.

On a Sunday afternoon when the family was gathered

around after lunch, it was decided that Khokon would study Medicine. He had procured the necessary grades in his exams to enable him to get into whichever stream he opted for. But not an architect, not an engineer, not a Chartered Accountant was he going to be. Jayant Kumar Guha (Khokon's name in the school register) was going to be a doctor, the uncles and his mother decided. Very essential to have a doctor in a family full of fifty-plus members. In fact every family needed a doctor these days, what with kidneys vanishing and all other kinds of malpractice rampant, said his elder uncle. Kakima, silent throughout the proceedings, felt a cold sense of foreboding at the announcement. Sharma Dadi sunning her pickles in the balcony above heard every word being spoken. She shook her head in distressed resignation. Khokon was not really required to utter a syllable on this occasion.

Khokon's first few days at the medical college hostel were unremarkable. A dehydrated looking senior had sauntered up to him on the second day with a cigarette hanging from his lips.

"I hear you are a Bengali. Are you a hep Bong or a mustard-oil Bong, Guho?" asked the boy, pronouncing his surname in the correct Bengali manner.

Khokon was nonplussed. While it was true that his mother plastered his head everyday with a hair oil that smelled of hibiscus flowers basking in the sun, it was also true that he listened to Pink Floyd into the early hours of the morning. But the boy seemed to be in too much of a hurry to wait for an answer.

"Call me if you have a problem, guru. They call me

Anjan Ray." In the first few weeks of college Khokon realised that he was different. He did not smoke, drink, pot, hash or have girlfriends like the others. Besides he dreamt in colour – in blazing vivid Kodak colour. It astonished him to know that most of the boys dreamt in black and white. Well, at least he seemed to have an edge over the others in this one matter. Black and white! How awful, he thought, watching night after night pass by like some old Alfred Hitchcock movie. Depressing, to say the least. He still dreamt his old dreams of floating down the stairs, breaking little bits of plaster on the way. And he still lay awake imagining galaxies outside galaxies outside galaxies till he fell asleep with a throbbing head.

Lacking in wit, muscles and repartee, Khokon became one of the most popular boys in the hostel. His room became the meeting ground for friends on Saturday nights. Singers sang on such occasions, guitarists strummed, boozards boozed, smokers smoked, junkies potted while hashers hashed. Khokon merely sat, watched and nibbled Jim-Jam biscuits. And the boys respected him tremendously for this. With the magnanimity of the young, each boy was too busy sculpting his own personality to bother about wrecking another's.

Khokon hated Medicine. The first day at the dissection table had brought on a bout of dizziness that made him flop down on the floor. And then the smell started following him. From the college and back to the hostel, to his room, to the mess, to the library ... the haunting nauseating smell of formalin. Having bones and a skull strewn around his room (for his orthopaedic studies) was also not really his style. Student lore had it that a second year student had hung himself in this very room years back. Monsoon winds had started shrieking at the windows. Khokon, scared of ghosts from early childhood, was too scared to even open his eyes at night. He just might see some transparent figure grinning at him flanked by his orthopaedic bones. He did not budge the whole night long, out of fear. He greeted the dawn with relief and a bursting bladder.

The weather was changing. Within and without. Breakers came crashing from the sea and washed over Khokon's seaside hostel. Dettol bottles and cologne vials could be heard smashing in the boys' rooms. There was a touch of yearning when voices sang to guitars in the blue twilit corridors. The warden taking quiet rounds at such times wondered whether hormones were at play or homesickness. Stories floated around. Of recession. Of jobless professionals. Of management graduates in well-placed jobs being given sudden farewell parties. Of medical specialists who languished in government hospitals till eternity. Never to afford matrimony. Who lived with their parents till middle-aged and bald. Never to afford a house of one's own.

Khokon was uneasy. It was his third miserable year of medical training. He went to the hostel terrace once in a while, all on his own. Sometimes the sea was gray and glassy with a film of mist all over. At such times the horizon seemed to merge seamlessly into the skies. There was a kind of timelessness about such moments. Khokon looking down at the road far below felt as if he was standing on the edge of some mysteriously attractive void and the slightest tilt of his heels would tip him headlong downwards ... down, down, down....

"Whatza doing guru?" Anjanda startled him from the back. "Planning to jump?" He patted Khokon's shoulder affectionately. "Just kidding!" Anjan Ray moved on.

It was a Sunday at Halfway House again, like so many Sundays before and so many more to come. The six-course meal went on till three in the afternoon. Kakima had surpassed herself trying to cook all of Khokon's favourite dishes on his weekend home. Afternoon had spilled into dusk without anyone really noticing. The girls were crowded at the far end of the room giggling over carrom.

"So! How are your studies progressing, Khokon?" asked his eldest uncle, deep-voiced.

This, thought Khokon frantically, this is the moment of truth. This was the opportunity that he had waited for. For years. To tell everybody that medical awakening had not come to him and wasn't ever likely to do so. That he did not want to be an engineer or a doctor or an architect. He just wanted to be. Like his favourite character Holden Caulfield maybe he could just sit on the grass at the edge of a cliff and prevent daft children from running right off the cliff. Nothing competitive, nothing demanding, just to be a catcher in the rye like Caulfield. Regressing further, he thought longingly of the little mermaid in his dog-eared childhood fairy-tale book. The little mermaid who eventually became a whiff of breeze, destined to blow for three hundred years cooling people's hot, flushed faces. What a wonderful vocation to have, thought Khokon wistfully. Never having to perform, never having to prove oneself, merely blowing around. He hated syringes, stethoscopes and scalpels; he wanted to scream at the uncles. All he wanted to do in life was to lie back and dream of the Aurora Borealis and listen to the wind in the trees.

Khokon's youngest uncle chose this moment to give a loud, long, blissful burp that he had been building up for the past hour. The moment was lost. Khokon felt defeated right up to his bone marrow. Talk turned to Osama Bin Laden, the Russians and the dog-bite-master risks of rearing terrorists. Pakistani politics hovered on the periphery of the conversation and voices were starting to get louder. When Khokon rose and slowly left the room unnoticed, the uncles could be heard arguing loudly over the validity of Marxism in the present day political scenario.

Last week, one of his uncles had come to visit him at the hostel with a friend and his daughter in tow. The owlish looking friend was introduced as the millionaire owner of a chain of undergarment shops. He was looking out for a prospective groom for his daughter. The daughter dimpling impishly informed him that she would like to marry a doctor. To Khokon, the introduction seemed to take on nightmarish overtones. Looking at his uncle's haggard hopeful face, it seemed to him as if an endless lineup of Guha ancestors were peering expectantly at him from behind his uncle – all of them gray, weary and financially challenged. All of them waiting for the first son in years to vindicate them by becoming a qualified medico with a brilliantly matched marriage to boot.

Khokon left for his hostel on Sunday night instead of the usual early Monday morning. At the hostel, the corridors were deserted and the rooms padlocked. Anjan Ray, the lone wolf was also not on the prowl tonight. He was away visiting relatives. Khokon switched on the tablelamp and sat down at his studytable. He read Sigmund Freud's *Interpretation of Dreams* till late into the night. He then pulled out a scalpel from the drawer, bent down, made a neat incision and settled back on his pillows to watch the sun rise over the sea. The crimson at the horizon matched the slowly spreading crimson on the bed-sheet. As he watched his faculties take wing like a bunch of gas balloons released suddenly, it struck him that he was no longer squeamish about blood.

When Jayanta Kumar Guha slit his wrist with his college scalpel, it was probably the only time he truly applied his medical knowledge.

THE OUTSIDER

Bubla Bose sat in a cane lounger on the balcony, sipping her early morning tea. She was wrapped up in shawls and mufflers to guard against the cool morning air. Dappled sunlight peeped through the surrounding foliage and lit up her gray-blue face. Last night had been quite bad. She had to be plugged with anti-histamines and inhalers midway through the night and had slept for a mere two hours propped up by pillows into a semi-sitting position. These severe asthma attacks were getting quite frequent of late and Bubla and her mother now calmly took it as a way of life.

There! There was the trio Bubla loved watching every weekday morning – Supriya, Sharmila and Malaika. All the three women were hurrying their respective children to the bus stop on the main road, a little way ahead. Their bodies were tense and tall with anticipated calamities and small string purses with emergency funds swung from their shoulders. Frequent calamities occurred in the form of forgotten Atlases, sports shoes missed on the appointed days, unscheduled urges to go to the bathroom.... All these things meant missing the school bus and having to frantically hail a taxi. Bubla watched the daily drama with the delicious delight of the aerial viewer. There! The buses were off with the children intact and the air echoed with much waving and screams of Bye! Byee! Byeee! Three sets of shoulders relaxed as the grim-faced thirtyish mothers suddenly metamorphosed into giggly, garrulous teenagers. This, thought Bubla sympathetically, was their hour of catharsis before they wandered off to their respective homes and worlds. And, to quote Supriya, became Cinderellas once more. Supriya never failed to look up and wave out to Bubla on her way home. She always seemed to have something saucy to say to the chronically sick spinster.

"Hi there Bubla! Come down and have a look at the mynahs – such pretty birds! One for sorrow, two for joy, three for letter, four for BOY! The early bird gets the boyfriend. Confucius said that."

"Confucius said all that?" smiled Bubla.

"Well, if he didn't he should have," said Supriya severely. "Why don't you join us in the mornings, Bubla? Gorgeous hunks jogging all over the place in shorts. Lovely sight and the best remedy for asthma."

Supriya glanced slyly at the adjacent windows for signs of the Titanic (her private name for Bubla's mother). There was nothing she enjoyed better than baiting Bose Mashima.

"Listen, Bubla," continued Supriya, "there is a Book Fair at the Reclamation Grounds. I'm going there this morning. Come along with me."

A visit to the Book Fair on a winter morning, thought Bubla ecstatically, why, wouldn't that be just wonderful? The wind on one's face, the lovely smell of old, yellowed, moth-eaten books, the exciting prospect of discovering some long forgotten author, hot tea, maybe even some of those evilly greasy samosas that were never allowed to get near her ... and of course, the one-woman entertainment show, Supriya, who was guaranteed to be the liveliest of companions.

"Bubla is going nowhere!" the words shot out like bullets into the air. Mrs. Bose moved into view after having been an invisible listener for some time. "She is allergic to dust and the grounds will be full of it. The air is too chilly besides. Bubla is much better off at home."

Mrs. Bose stood in the balcony, arms akimbo, eyes angry and cold. There was a brief duel of glances between the two women, which Mrs. Bose won as usual. Supriya shrugged and sauntered away, humming some tuneless song.

When Supriya and Mrs. Bose had first met six years back, it had been a classic case of hate at first sight. The champion of the downtrodden and the chief cheerleader of the underdogs right from her college days, Supriya had no difficulty summing up Mrs. Bose at the first lightning glance. A frustrated, domineering, overpossessive mother, thought the adjective-happy Supriya, who had with the skilful use of psychological tactics turned her youngest-born into a hypochondriac. Captive for life to breathlessness, never to even dream of freedom.

Mrs. Bose on the other hand, after glacially acknowledging the introduction had spat out the word "taansh" venomously behind Supriya's jeans-clad, pert-bottomed retreating figure. The word "taansh" in her husband's opinion epitomized the resentment of the collective Bengali "bhadralok" psyche against the once prevalent British rule. According to Mr. Bose (who spent a lot of time mulling over such matters), it was applied by the opinionated Bengali gentry to the swarms of Anglo-Indians who mushroomed in the wake of the British. For Mrs. Bose on the other hand, whose sensibilities were sculpted and honed by Rabindrasangeet and Saratchandra literature, by mustard fish and sweet red yoghurt, who oiled and watered her head everyday (to keep a cool head), who smeared vermillion generously into her centre-parted hair, who wore blazing white bangles coupled with deep red coral ones, the slang term "taansh" had a wider spectrum of implication. To her mind it made a wide clean sweep of unacceptable things like too red lipstick, too tight clothes, too loud laughter, short, frizzy hair infested with lice, promiscuous leanings and the habit of eating bread at mealtimes.

When Bubla sat in her chair in the balcony every morning, Supriya looked up and saw a wistful face, eager to live and not merely exist. Bubla's mother on the other hand, looking at Bubla from her kitchen end saw a pinched-looking profile, gray with the lack of oxygen and who needed to be pampered, cosseted and medicated with clockwork precision. The perspectives of the two women who loved Bubla equally seemed to strangely lack congruence and it was as if the frontal Bubla was quite different from the lateral Bubla.

Supriya had infuriated Mrs. Bose further by once suggesting that Bubla's condition did not need either Allopathy, Homeopathy, telepathy or sympathy. All she needed was a hot, virile hunk of a husband and a house of her own.

Mrs. Bose's marriage was not a success. In the very first year of marriage Mr. Bose had discovered the many virtues of the betel-leaf. He also made the important discovery that a paan in the mouth was worth a dozen in the pocket. Every evening on the way back home from work, he bought himself an exciting triangular packet of stained newspaper that contained his preciously guarded getaway secret. For popping a paan into his mouth after his shower and tea blanketed him against the entire hostile world. Unpleasant facts of life like the children's report card postmortems, household budgeting, in-law visits were all waved away grandly by an eloquent forefinger pointed at a loaded cheek. A mouthful of crimson betel-leaf juice threatening to spill out at the slightest opportunity was an effective determent to conversation of any kind, he found to his delight. He also discovered that erecting a high citadel of newspapers, along with the paan-chewing rendered him invisible as well as speechless. He read each news item meticulously, repeating the obituary section a couple of times and made the papers stretch on till dinner time. For years he existed alternately buried under accounts at his office desk and buried voluntarily in a newspaper sarcophagus at home.

A benign tumour in the mouth at the age of fifty-two frightened the wits out of Mr. Bose. He gave up paan-chewing with alarmed alacrity. For the first time in years he lowered his bi-focals and blinked around like a bald, bewildered Bengali-speaking Rip Van Winkle. He was shocked at what he saw. He saw two belligerent young men glaring at him in place of the ice cream licking sons in shorts whom he remembered. And an irate, overweight, menopausal woman who snapped in place of the docile beauty he had married. The boys left for foreign shores a year later and never ever turned back to look homewards. Mrs. Bose, emotionally deprived for years, now channellized her ample energies towards their youngest asthmatic daughter Bubla. Her love and devotion towards Bubla so awesomely resembled a tidal wave at times that friends and relatives were often alarmed and words like "pathological" and "obsessive," unuttered, seemed to hover in every mind.

Mr. Bose's retirement coincided rather unhappily with his domestic awakening. Mrs. Bose now faced the awful prospect of having a suddenly attentive, middle-aged husband all over the house, all day long. She wasn't sure at times, that the paan-newspaper days weren't really better. After years of non-communication the couple really had nothing to say to one another and no established code of behaviour to fall back on. Mrs. Bose like generations of her predecessors took to barking out only necessary instructions at her husband, rather in the manner of a master calling his dog to heel. And guilty of years of neglect, Mr. Bose immediately jumped into waggy-tailed obedience.

At the age of nine, the (till then) hale and hearty Bubla had come home from school at recess time accompanied by a worried looking teacher. Acute breathlessness had struck Bubla in the Mathematics period and she had to be rushed home. This was Bubla's first attack of asthma. Gradually, the intensity of the attacks increased as did the frequency. In a couple of years' time Bubla had turned into a semi-invalid and had to be at all times protected against dust, pollen, weather changes, too much joy and excessive sorrow. She lived in a twilight world of chess, solitaire, books, pills and inhalers. Deprived of socializing opportunities (too much excitement), outings (too much pollen), movies (too much bad breath), Bubla devised a living technique all her own. She sat at the window or the balcony and watched life go by. She threw herself into every creature that passed below her house. She felt a cow's agony when she mooed raggedly for her lost calf, she felt the office-goer's fatigue in her bones when he trudged back home at dusk, and she tasted lipstick on her mouth when teenaged girls swung past. She lived life by projection.

Bubla's favourite pastime was to sit in a dark car all alone when her parents got down to shop, and watch the play of neon lights on peoples' faces. She played a little game with herself. That young man loping down the road in tight jeans and sneakers, walkman at his ears, now what was he going back to? A tubelight-lit bare paying guest accommodation in all probability, she thought, littered with books, cassettes and other paraphernalia, smelling of unwashed socks and two-minute noodles. The woman in the black burqa now, showing only exquisitely fair hands, would probably go back to a home teeming with children and relatives and smelling of high-fat cooking and meat. A dozen pairs of footwear would lie in confusion at the doorway, she thought, while the woman in black served her family with features and emotions safely concealed behind a curtain of black. It was a wonderful guessing game that kept her absorbed for long lengths of time. She sat and watched raptly as joy, cunning, greed and angst stalked the neon-lit streets. Not even the mosquitoes invading the car at sundown bothered her at such times.

Bubla never really took up any vocation. She spent the morning hours doing cross-stitch and the evening ones reading Mills and Boon romances. She always wore a light cardigan, even in the heat of the summers. In winter she wore quantities of woollens, complete with a monkey-cap and muffler. Only the Polar bears and the huskies, according to Supriya, were missing.

Bubla was going to be inducted into the yogic fold. An ex-colleague of Mr. Bose who came calling one morning, explained how yoga besides elevating the soul also elevated the lung power. Mr. Bose, suitably impressed, got home a tall, lanky young man a few days later to initiate Bubla into the ways of the ancient wise men. And Tushar Walhawalkar entered the Bose household for the first time.

Walhawalkar chose morning as the time of instruction. Bubla who went blue in the face at the first session alarming her teacher considerably, slowly learnt how to breathe from the navel, how to blank out her mind into nothingness and how to loosen every muscle and resemble a corpse. Once in a while she opened her eyes mid-exercise to find her teacher staring at her fixedly. Good heavens, she thought going breathless all over again, was the man getting ATTRACTED to her? She knew that she should be flattered – being 29, unmarried and with no chances of matrimony in the near future. But Walhawalkar looked so much like Dolly Mashi's pet poodle that she felt vaguely giggly.

Supriya watched the proceedings with smug satisfaction as Walhawalkar bounded past her window every morning, brushed, brilliantined, perfumed and with love-light in his eyes. Madame Titanic was in for a surprise collision one of these days, she thought gleefully. She prayed hard that Bubla's courage should not give way at the last minute. "How's the yoga thing going, Bubla?" she asked one day linking arms with her friend. "Your yoga teacher is kind of cute you know. Reminds me of Winnie the Pooh."

Bubla stiffened, pulling her arm out of her friend's grasp. "I haven't really noticed his looks," she said coldly. "I try and concentrate on the deep-breathing."

"Oh, come off it Bubla!" exploded Supriya. "Wake up and start living. Or are you planning to wheeze away your entire life with your rump turned to reality? Can't you see Walhawalkar loves you and is your lifeline to freedom? Do you see yourself ever getting better in that hellhole of a house with Mamma breathing down your neck every minute? Why, I believe she is the biggest allergen of your life. In fact there are times when she gives ME hay fever!"

Supriya stopped short. Maybe she had said too much. Bubla stood frozen, breathing hard. She then turned on her heel wordlessly and marched off, offended beyond words. She was seething from within. Really, Supriya went too far sometimes. What on earth was she trying to imply, that she was ... what was that awful word now ... yes, MALINGERING? That her

21

condition that left her gasping for breath, blue in the nails with pinched bronchioles and her entire system yearning for a wholesome supply of oxygen was ... what was that horrific term ... PSYCHOSOMATIC?

Well, it was true in a way wasn't it, said a traitorous voice within her. Wasn't it infinitely more comfortable being a ringside viewer than a participant? Wasn't it so much cosier living life through others rather than to be oneself? Never to have to take decisions, never to be exposed to hurt, never to confront, never to have to cope....

Bubla sat lost in thought in her usual chair in the stillness of the late afternoon. Traffic honked – a faraway sound. Walhawalkar was not bad looking, she thought, just a little vague looking. And he may be just a yoga teacher but he was the only child of a man who owned a three-storey house (built from winning a crossword puzzle in the sixties). The rent alone would ensure comfortable living. She would have to learn how to cook "varan," pressure-cooker rice and exquisitely thin Maharashtrian chapatis if she married Tushar. Having eaten only sweet-water fish all her life, she would have to now venture into frying sea-water fish which by all accounts stank to high heaven....

Supriya watched Walhawalkar, stiff and self-conscious in a bright new shirt complete with fluttering price tag enter the Boses' house. He held a dainty little marigold in his hand and had chosen an hour when the senior Boses would be haggling over salmons a mile away. Supriya guessed that today was the day of reckoning. She sat with her chin in her hands, immobile, her television script lying forgotten before her.

Never in her life had she prayed so hard as she did for her sick friend now. Oh, my God! She leapt up suddenly, scattering sheets of paper all around. Mashima was coming back – an unscheduled early return!

Walhawalkar emerged an hour later. He looked utterly dejected and droopy, like the marigold in his sweaty hand. He went around the corner at a quick pace without looking back even once. Even the back of his neck looked defeated.

Bubla Bose sat in the balcony watching dusk gather. Wood smoke rose from the shanty towns near the horizon. Children were at play. Evening sounds had a kind of echoing quality that heralded the arrival of winter. Bubla adjusted her shawl and settled down more comfortably in her armchair. So would she sit maybe for years to come. Destined to be an eternal spectator and an outsider forever. And maybe not.

It was really nobody's business after all.

THE JOURNEY

Noon weighed heavily on Halfway House. A cicada-touched silence hung over the building while traffic honked distantly. The house stood quiet and dreaming. Afternoon sun filtered dustily over silent landings while in the darkly curtained rooms fans whirred softly.

Mrs. Banerjee Senior was intensely contemptuous towards this thing called a siesta. She virtuously embroidered away the noon hours, looking up once in a while. There! There was the postman coming in all his gangly glory. Just one lavender-coloured envelope for her it seemed. She slit it open with a sense of delicious anticipation. Letters (other than those wretched ones about expiring fixed deposits) always filled her with excitement. This one was from her niece Priyam.

"Dear Dolly Mashi," it began, "I am back at Berkeley at last. Boy, am I glad to be back! You asked me about the latter part of my vacation when I rang you up from

Heathrow. The first fortnight with all of you at Mumbai was such a blast but the latter part of my Gujarat holiday, Mashi, I would like to forget forever...."

Priyam came out of the bamboo grove. It was like coming out of church. The bamboo grove with its tall columns of bamboo plants, high ceiling of feathery leaves blocking out all sunlight save an eerie green light that filtered all over, gave her the creeps. It was lovely emerging out into bright hot sunshine. Stretches of tall waving grass lined the road and a million little wild yellow blossoms danced in the breeze in true Wordsworth style. Gosh, the haversack sure was heavy. She had arrived in Mumbai with just one extra pair of jeans other than the ones she wore and a couple of skimpy tops. She was now returning with mirror-work skirts that seemed to weigh tons, khadi kurtas, pickles, pappads and nearly half of Gujarat, she thought wryly. But her friends at Berkeley would murder her if she didn't....

She flopped down by the road exhausted, and pulled out a bottle of distilled water. God bless the gent who had thought of inventing purified water, she thought. A couple of years in the US and your resistance got shot to pieces. "You phirangs!" her cousins and Supriya boudi were always ribbing her contemptuously. "You have to just step off the aircraft and buckle down within minutes with dysentery, diarrhoea, malaria, typhoid ... the works!" A soft drink with meals was another habit that one's desi relatives could never stomach. She remembered Dolly Mashi exploding when she timidly asked for a Coke at lunch.

"What! Coke with shukto and doi-mach? The idea!"

She had withered Priyam with what was popularly termed the "Dangerous Dolly Look." It was another matter that to counteract the glare she invariably gave the recipient an extra scoop of rasmalai or whatever sinfully delicious dessert she had up her sleeve.

Priyam lay back on a carpet of wild flowers. The breeze flirted around with her shoulder length hair as she nibbled on a sweet juicy blade of grass. Today, she thought dreamily, today was a day to just drift along. A day to lie back and give shapes and names to clouds. Today was a day to be irresponsible and have unhygienic ice-lollies bought at tiny roadside stalls. And lie back and remember beautiful retro songs. Today, she thought lazily, was a day for meandering aimlessly and be just a little insane. "Priyambahen, are you going to the bus depot?" the urgent-voiced question broke into her reverie. Harmeshbhai stood over her, tense and taut. There was no sign of the usual indulgent smile reserved for the pretty, eccentric, US-returned Priyam.

"Why ... yes," Priyam sat up quickly, grass all over her hair.

"You'd better hurry up. There's trouble brewing."

Trouble? In sleepy little Valod, the land of Gandhiji, thought Priyam bewildered.

A group of moving people suddenly seemed to dot the horizon. Harmeshbhai looked uneasy. He gave her a quick searching glance from head to toe.

"Thank God you're wearing jeans," he said tersely. "Get onto my scooter. I'll take you to the bus-stop."

They were then speeding past the mustard fields. Behind them a shout seemed to ring out and Harmeshbhai quickly picked up speed. They stopped near a group of people gathered uneasily under a neem tree. A woodpecker chucked in perfect rhythm somewhere in the quiet mid-morning hour. Snatches of conversation wafted out into the still air.

"Trains have stopped. Some problem somewhere ... a bogey burnt with passengers inside...."

"They are stopping people...."

"Burning buses...."

A battered white Maruti van drew up and the driver got down.

"I'm going to Mumbai. Safest thing to do," he announced. "Anyone wants to come along?"

There was a clamour of voices as five people including Priyam scrambled into the van. A figure lay on the floor of the van, wrapped up in a dirty bed-sheet. Priyam was squeezed tight into a corner. The hefty elbow of a plump Gujarati woman was lodged into her ribs and the supine figure's head was practically on her feet. There was a babble of voices within the van.

"Riots ... roadblocks...."

"'People gutting houses, cars...."

Fragments of conversation filtered into her befuddled brain.

The figure on the floor suddenly groaned, the driver of the van, Mansukhbhai, glanced back worriedly.

"He is very very ill. Cardiac asthma. Needs urgent medical help," he said. Priyam bent down and flipped the sheet off the man's face. She knew a thing or two about asthma. Her grandmother had died of it and she had also seen Bubladi's suffering at Halfway House. "Air!" she said firmly, "he needs air."

She propped him up using her haversack as a pillow and opened all the windows of the van. Slowly and with circular movements she started massaging his chest. The old man coughed a loud phlegmatic sound in the small confines of the car. The rest of the passengers crowded around, concerned and eager to help the stranger.

"Hamidmiya, are you feeling a little better now?" Mansukhbhai glanced back briefly from his driving.

An invisible shaft of lightning seemed to split the van into two. Like static electricity felt with the rising of one's hair but never seen. Three people recoiled back in revulsion. Only Rupalbahen and Priyam were left to manage the gasping Hamid. "There's a crowd coming," said Mansukhbhai suddenly, agitated. "Cover him up."

They covered him up hurriedly. His nose would have to be left open, thought Priyam agonizedly, but his hennaed beard would have to be covered. Rupalbahen opened her purse, grabbed Priyam and planted a bindi the size of a California sunset on her forehead. "Bindi with jeans!" protested Priyam.

"Quiet!" commanded Mansukhbhai, terrifyingly low-voiced.

A group of men with saffron head sashes had stopped their van. They came around to the back, eyes scanning every face minutely. "Who is that?" asked the tallest of the lot, pointing to the figure in the bed-sheet.

"My servant," said Kantabahen quickly. "Has malarial fever and needs to see a doctor fast."

The men fell back, nodding.

"Retaliation is beginning everywhere. One of my men will ride with you for protection," said the tall man who seemed to be the leader of the small group.

One of his men got into the front seat next to Mansukhbhai. His thigh bulged with the flash of some sharp metal. There was a deathlike silence within the van. Priyam saw glances of pure hatred shafted towards the supine figure. "Do you know this area?" asked the man in saffron. "I don't. I'm from Baroda."

Mansukhbhai shook his head. "I'm not too sure of this region either," he said worriedly. "There are certain pockets we have to be careful about. But who is going to guide me?"

"I will," said Priyam into the silence. Shocked faces turned towards her.

"I have been here before," she lied, strong-voiced.

She looked into Hamidmiya's eyes pleadingly. The old eyes weary with the lack of oxygen reassured her. Yes, said the eyes, I will guide you.

"Do we go left here?" asked Mansukhbhai at a turning.

No, warned the eyes.

"No, go straight on," directed Priyam from the back.

"A crossing coming up," said Mansukhbhai a little later.

A gnarled finger pointed shakily from within the sheet.

"Go right," said Priyam confidently.

Saffron-head shifted in his seat restlessly, glancing backwards. Danger. Only the eyes would have to do the talking. The eyes rolled upwards and then stayed fixed straight ahead. No movement at all. No turns that meant, straight, straight, straight....

The van burst onto the Express Highway like a bat escaping from hell.

Eighty, seventy, sixty.... The speedometer relaxed as they flew past, all eyes focused towards Mumbai. The horizon behind was lit up with stray flashes of orange fire and plumes of black smoke as villages and sanity burned in unison.

They were entering Dahisar now. Back to safety, thought Priyam, back to freedom, back to sanity, back to Mumbai. Mansukhbhai drove his van straight into the courtyard of a small, rustic teashop. Priyam and the others tumbled out of the van, limbs stiff with latent fear. Relief was palpable on every face. Saffron-head declined tea, touched his forehead to them and vanished in the direction of Gujarat. Tea at last, thought Priyam.

"Hamidmiya, get up," Priyam patted the old shoulder affectionately. "You saved us today! Get up and have some hot ginger tea."

There was no answer.

"Hamidmiya, are you alright...Hamidmiya...?"

They gathered around the old bony figure, shaking him frantically. But Hamidmiya did not answer. He was as cold as the winters in Gujarat, having been dead for some time now.

A HOUSE WITH A VIEW

Malaika Mukherjee hated her nose. It was an exquisitely aquiline affair – a nose to be proud of in her parents' opinion. But Malaika would rather have had one of those tiny retrousse noses that turned Hollywood heroes weak at the knees. She firmly believed that her nose was too big and too sharp for her lean, clean-cut face. The same deep-seated congenital desire for symmetry flowed onto other things. At the age of three she was seen tugging at crooked carpets, straightening askew picture frames and checking the entire house for upturned slippers. Aesthetics and symmetry were not just a need but a passion with Malaika.

When Malaika married Mukul Ganguly, it was a perfect merger of castes, complexions and complexities. (The matrimonial advertisement in the papers had read tall, fair graduate Bengali Brahmin girl under 25 wanted for tall, handsome 34-year-old Probasi Bengali Brahmin engineer holding a job in a multinational company). With a delicious sense of anticipation Malaika waited to enter her new home after marriage. Her very own home, uncluttered and uninterrupted. Uncluttered by mothers who insisted on hanging godly pictures the size of hoardings in the drawing room and uncluttered by fathers who insisted on dumping cigarettes, lighters, snuff boxes, open crossword pages and a dozen bi-focals on the coffee table. And expecting others to treat these items with reverence besides! Mukul, being just an engineer from a capitation college from the back of beyond (a fact that Malaika used skillfully in squashing many an argument in her favour) was quelled into submission on the very first day. No Hawaii slippers to be thrown higgledy-piggledy, no ashtrays spilling over with cigarette butts and no mangled Sunday papers drifting all over the house. Everything was going to be just shipshape and sparkling.

When Malaika had her first look at the flat in Halfway House, her heart hit her sandals with a resounding crash. The company flat allotted to them was designed rather like a railway train that had run away with itself, thought Malaika. A long corridor ran unimaginatively along a series of rooms. The windows of each room uniformly faced east. A great view on the east would probably have salvaged the house somewhat. But at nose-to-nose distance was the back of another building. The array of rear windows of this building showed an interesting variety of views. A window in line with Malaika's prospective house had grubby-looking laundry hung up on a line while another kitchen window showed an old blackened pressure cooker whistling away to glory. A shabbily dressed, old, white-haired lady stood at a window gazing vacantly into space while at yet another window a muscle-bound man in a vest did weights. This, thought Malaika grimly, is going to be tough. A clothesline on the fourth floor had a sunset orange sari fluttering in the November wind but Malaika was too distracted to notice this pretty sight.

What had she dreamt of all these years? A house of her own – gleaming with floors that reflected happy faces, corners spilling with potted plants, cane loungers in unexpected nooks to fall into with a book and forget the world. Windows opening onto sun, sky and breeze so that one woke up with the feeling of tumbling into space and tree tops. Rain, storms and seasons passing by at touching distance.

That had been six and a half years back. Her children were now five and three. Honestly, Mukul was the most thickheaded of husbands. Even a man with a blindfold would realize that they needed to move to a bigger and better place. But husbands! Women are from Venus, sure, sure, thought Malaika sourly, but MEN, (that weird species) were from some other galaxy altogether. Closeted in his swanky, air-conditioned office all day long and coming home only to eat and sleep, what would he know about her plight? Why, only the other day when Bimal Meshomoshai visited her for the first time after her marriage, Mrs. Awasthi across chose that very day to do her weekly lingerie washing. And what a view awaited poor old Mesho! A dozen oversized underwear waving in the winter wind. The horror of it all! It had taken all of

Malaika's manipulative skills to keep Mesho's back turned to the window. And these wretched builders! They seemed to know nothing about cross ventilation and straight edges. Why, every corner in this claustrophobic house seemed to miss a right angle by a wide margin!

Mukul's Mejo Mama and Mamima were descending on them next week besides. Now where on earth was she going to do her late night ironing for school? The ironing table would be chockfull of bottles of Homeopathy pills, antacids, laxatives, blood pressure pills and a hundred other bottles that the mamas carted around with them. Mama and Mamima would get up at the crack of dawn and station themselves in the living room sofa to watch the early morning school-leaving proceedings. And her children would sprout ten thumbs in place of two. They would expect early morning tea and biscuits (only Marie, nothing greasy at their age, thank you), empty bathrooms (bladder control was slightly poor at that age, heh, heh, heh). The children would miss the school bus every other day and would have to be dropped off at school. Mukul, of course, would be the charming, gushing nephew which was easy to be when you were leaving home in an hour's time. And those five course lunches that she would have to organize now, she fumed to herself. Something bitter to begin, a fried item with the dal, two vegetables, sweet-water fish curry, a sweet-sour chutney, freshly set yoghurt (not the overnight kind that could be bad for their delicate old throats), sweetmeats – the syrupy kind they were used to in Kolkata and not the dry as dust non-Bengali variety that would make the poor darlings gag. And for which, thought Malaika viciously, she would have to drive a good mile to the nearest Bengali sweet shop. All this poppy seed eating, muttered Malaika angrily to herself, had sent the collective Bengali mindset into partial paralysis. Look at how evolved the Probasi Bengali was, now. Why, he could happily make a meal out of a packet of soup and instant noodles!

"Mukul! Are you listening?" she snapped. "We just have to move to a bigger place. What about those people in the 'C' Wing who were having a distress sale? They were due to leave for Dubai in a couple of months...."

"Siiiiiiix!" screamed Mukul leaping up into the air. A collective cry of joy rose up from the buildings all around. Sachin Tendulkar had once again done India proud.

"About the flat in the 'C' Wing...." started Malaika hopefully again. "Sshhh! Three balls to go and five runs to make. Don't talk, don't move, and don't even think!"

Malaika felt an irrepressible urge to hit her husband on the head with something hard. Something in the line of a stump or a bat. Or even a season ball would do. Why was it that there was always something urgent happening to divert Mukul when the talk turned to buying a new house? And why did her normally attentive husband get all absent-minded and vacant-eyed when it came to discussing home loans?

Malaika slammed out of the room and flopped down on her bed in the bedroom. Not that Mukul was likely to notice, besotted as he was with the game and particularly with India playing today. She would check out her missed calls on the answering machine. That might just make her mercury level drop.

"Hi friend-who-never-answers!" quipped the answering machine. "When you've done with boiling potatoes and washing bottoms, I've got a great offer lined up for you. Ring back soon. Toodle-doo. Reema."

Thank god for school friends like Reema, thought Malaika over lunch the next day, who never change, remain on the same wavelength and speak the same language for years. Reema came straight to the point as was her habit of long.

"My husband Sidharth is going into interiors. He needs someone with class, great aesthetics and taste for the showroom decoration. About four hours of cushy work five days a week and fantastic remuneration at the end of it. Can't think of anyone better than you, M. Do say yes," said Reema.

"But my kids –"

"Are old enough!"

"My husband –"

"Is positively ancient!"

"My maids –"

"Are better off without you!"

Malaika giggled. Could one ever say no to Reema? Come to think of it, with the mornings free, it wasn't such a bad idea....

Unlimited resources, sprawling spaces and a free rein to the imagination. It was cloudburst over a desert. Furniture would have to have the right kind of setting, thought Malaika excitedly in her first week at work, window displays would have to match seasons and festivals. Life became full of exciting things like terracotta and ceramic ware, tie-and-dye fabrics and wrought iron furniture. An unpolished bullock-cart wheel was imaginatively transformed into a centre table while unbaked earthen pots stood at attention in the ethnique corner. Muted lights bounced off polished wood surfaces on the French furniture floor and shoppers could almost smell French wines and perfumes. Stained glass partitions strategically placed had sunlight filtering through them and splaying into multi-hued beams that along with the gleaming silent shop floor reminded strollers of ancient Italian churches. Malaika scoured around for the right indoor plants. She hated all things artificial and plastic. So feathery ferns it was for the rustic corner and stiff rubber plants for the French one. A vibrant scarlet Poinsettia set off a Chippendale counter while money plants adorned a rosewood cabinet. Honestly, thought Reema admiringly, walking in one day, that woman could wreak pure magic. Just some weeks back, a leading women's magazine had featured Malaika as one of the most promising window designers and, thought Reema generously, the praise was well deserved.

Window displays fascinated Malaika. During Diwali, she strung up glittering little lights with invisible threads giving the impression of a hundred fireworks frozen mid-explosion. Little lamps with safe electric flames dotted the shop floor, lighting up shoppers' eyes and faces with a happy golden glow.

Christmas was a fortnight away and she could hardly think of anything else. She would have a cool colour theme maybe? Twinkling little lights in blues, greens and mauves. A half-light in which inhibitions would vanish, hidden desires emerge, and every face lit up with the green-blue glitter would appear to be that of a friend.

Strange how her house no longer bothered Malaika. No longer did laundry spilling out of inadequately sized cupboards threaten to stifle her. The Awasthi vests with holes in the armpits drying on the clothesline across no longer roused her to a fury. She now saw the house through Mukul's eyes. No longer a destination, it was merely a stopover for lodging and boarding on a journey leading elsewhere.

Mukul Ganguly was a worried man. His wife had stopped nagging for a new house. Malaika's chronic complaining was a sound that he had got habituated to over the years. It had a comfortable, repetitive quality to it like the news being read in the background all day long. This sudden silence unnerved him. And she went around with this goofy, happy, other-world expression besides. Was there some man on the scene? Really, it was most disturbing!

The children left for their annual visit to their grandparents in May and the two of them were left on their own for a few weeks. Mukul was going to cook the Sunday dinner. The menu was simple. Instant soup out of a packet, noodles with vegetables and bread pudding – an amateur's dinner. Which was alright since dinner was only a prelude to the main issue – Mukul's dramatic announcement. Malaika, who had been ordered out of the kitchen, sat on the sofa gazing at the full rising moon. It was spectacularly big, both golden and silver in impartial proportions. It lit up the Awasthi's building softly, making even the drainpipes and the waterproofing look romantic. What were those lines from her favourite poem in school?

"Slowly, silently now the moon, walks the night in her silver shoon. Such wonderful imagery ... Walter de la Mare, wasn't it?" thought Malaika dreamily.

Mukul was clattering away in the kitchen, trying to inexpertly organize coffee.

"This way and that she peers and sees, silver fruit upon silver trees," recited Malaika softly to herself. She sat up suddenly with suppressed excitement. "Why! I must have a pure silver window theme for Christmas! But of course! How could it be otherwise?" she thought, nearly jumping with joy. "Malaika!" announced Mukul importantly, standing at the doorway, coffee-tray in hand, "I've booked a flat!" "Uh-oh ... good, good," muttered Malaika absent-mindedly. "I'll have silver orbs hanging at corners, silver streamers, silver spangles and silver stars all over," she planned excitedly.

"MALAIKA! I've booked a 3 BHK house!" repeated Mukul a trifle louder. The words did not seem to be registering on his wife.

"Loads of white fleecy cotton with clear glass droplets reminding shoppers of white Christmases abroad and friends and relatives long lost to distant foreign lands...." thought Malaika.

"Sliding powder-coated windows, stainless steel sink, built-in cabinets...." announced Mukul proudly.

"And in the centre, lit up tenderly, a crystal reindeer pulling a timeless crystal sledge...." thought Malaika happily.

"1200 square feet, granite floors, concealed wiring...." continued Mukul.

"Now how did the poem end? Yes, 'And moveless fish in

the water gleam, by silver reeds in a silver stream.' Wonderful!" finished Malaika with smug satisfaction.

"Our new house...." started Mukul and petered off perplexed, coffee tray still in hand, mouth slightly open. His wife did not answer, did not seem to be listening and did not remotely seem to care.

Malaika Ganguly had moved on.

THE GHOSTWRITER

The telephone rang shrilly. Sharmila was reclining on a sofa, legs hooked over the sides, newspapers strewn all over her stomach and a coffee cup balanced precariously on her left thigh. The boys were away at school, Partho was on tour, the maids had still not trooped in and this was the hour of bliss. Groaning, she disentangled herself from the newspapers and reached out for the phone. It was Supriya.

"Listen!" Supriya began urgently, "I have a problem. Maloy's brother Indranil has to be bumped off. He is a nerd, never steps out of the house and so a car accident is out of question. Suicide doesn't fit in comfortably into the scheme of things and it had better not be a heart attack. He is only twenty-two. Think, think, think. And get back to me pronto." Click. Silence.

Sharmila sighed. She was used to these entirely one-sided bits of conversation from Supriya. A scriptwriter for a popular soap serial showing on a leading television channel, Supriya's life was fraught with crisis situations where characters from the serial had to be killed, married, kidnapped or sent to far-away places with disconcerting suddenness. Whims, availability and pregnancies of actors played havoc with a scriptwriter's life, Supriya had confessed morosely to Sharmila one day. Sharmila, with her fertile imagination was the best person to turn to in such predicaments as she invariably came up with quick satisfactory ways of bailing out her friend.

Sharmila rose and slowly started gathering scattered laundry clothes from the floor and the bright sun outside seemed to dim somewhat. The chicken would have to be defrosted, she thought wearily. She would make chilli chicken for lunch, she decided, the children hadn't had chilli chicken for quite a while now and it was a dish they simply loved. It was when she was trying to cut spring onions microscopically small without chopping her fingers in the bargain that the phone trilled shrilly again. The kitchen was bathed in soft warm morning sunlight. It lit up the orange colouring of the carrots, the emerald gleam of capsicums and bounced off the red turgid curves of tomatoes. It gently lit up Sharmila's hair, giving her tired, thin face a halo of gold. And all-pervading was the homely smell of onions and garlic cooking together. Now what on earth was one to do with the hapless Indranil? A sozzled Indranil reaching out for a swig of antacid in the middle of the night and gulping down Dettol instead, maybe? Did Dettol kill, wondered Sharmila hazily, or had it better be

Tincture Iodine? The ringing of the phone registered on her abstracted mind only a while later, scattering her homicidal plans in a million directions. It was her niece Nikki.

"Mamima!" cried Nikki, sounding desperate, "I'm an RJ for a radio program tonight. Theme is retro-music, colours and psychology. Help! The Beatles, Engelbert and such-like with lots and lots of psycho-babble. Mamima, help me puh-leeeese. Have my draft ready. I'll ring up in an hour's time. Ciao!"

Sharmila sighed again. That blasted chilli chicken would have to wait. She pulled out a dog-eared grocery pad and placed it over the microwave oven. "Think pink, think opium, think sepia labyrinths of the mind," she wrote, "visualize the blue, blue, blue of Spanish eyes and separation. Tonight, dear listeners, we get you the age of flower power, the spirit of the bohemians, soul...."

When Sharmila was six, her mental faculties had burst into life like the cosmos exploding. She started responding to sights, sounds, smells and that ambiguous thing called atmosphere with a kind of sensitivity and urgency that frightened her mother at times. Once, at the age of seven, after lying in a trance for an hour, she had leapt upon her grandfather with cannibalistic fervour.

"Dadu! How nice and BROWN you smell!" she had exclaimed, little nose and mouth buried into the old man's shoulder. "Smell BROWN, dear child?" the old man had quavered confusedly. Decades later, Sharmila was to remember the warm brown smell of snuff, old age and love. Sometimes, as a child, she would lie for hours viewing the world through one of her mother's semi-precious stones that came loose from brooches and rings. The amethyst was a favourite. Through it she saw a world that was suffused with a strange and wonderful light, where it was neither day nor night, where everything seemed enchanted and all exciting possibilities had the trick of coming true. She wrote her first poem at the age of five, a fifteen-line affair about a chocolate factory run by midgets. Her poem was circulated all around the classrooms in school, firmly establishing her reputation as a writer in the making. The genteel teachers of the all girls school were delighted. They were not wasting their breath manufacturing batches of bimbettes. Some of them, thank god, could actually think!

Incongruously, she opted for Science subjects in college. This was mainly because all good girls at the time chose Science to specialise in and any other option subtly implied that the girl was fast. On graduating, she acquiesced to marriage for the same very reason – to remain an upright citizen, doing the right thing at the right time at all times.

After marriage, Sharmila turned juggler. With a singleness of purpose she tossed around roles, duties and skills with a competence that amazed her sometimes. She took impartial turns at being a wife, a mother, a daughter, a daughter-in-law, cook, cleaner and hostess. She was a wonderful listener besides. She had a chameleon's ability to merge with the surroundings. She could, at a moment's notice, become wall, vase, drapery or crystal. The speaker, meanwhile, oblivious to her soothing non-presence laid himself bare before her. She sat, listened, absorbed and became a little of that other person. Sometimes, by the end of the day she had problems remembering who she really was.

Strangely, after the first few years of marriage, Sharmila's vocabulary seemed to dry up. Whether it was post-pregnancy hormones or the all-year-round influx of in-laws, she could never comprehend. Once in a while, a surge of words or a glimmer of poetry seemed to flash somewhere in the spaces of her mind like a mirage but on closer inspection all that was visible was arid wasteland.

And then started the trickle of requests. An essay to be helped with, a school level poem to be composed, a concert script here, a colony skit there.... Years later, struggling between chilli chicken, Strawberry Fields and forensic details, she felt an old familiar stirring within her. The urge to write. To throw caution, spoons, ladles to the wind and just write. Write without parameters, without space, time and age constraints and above all, write for herself. In the last fortnight, she had written an inaugural speech for a local corporator not too comfortable with the Queen's English, drafted a statement of purpose for a neighbour's son hoping to make it to Michigan University, and helped a schoolboy with a long cheerless poem on nuclear warfare meant for the school magazine. Yah! It was time to get cracking and start writing for herself. But how on earth was she to get started? Having been duty-alive and brain-dead for years now, it was going to be difficult igniting fires in the spaces between her ears. Long back, in her early teens, she had seen herself as a major writer in the making and dreamt of writing that one book that would stop the globe mid-axis. In a moment of weakness and on a hot summer afternoon of confidences she had revealed her yearnings to a distant cousin. Her cousin Teertha had patted her very kindly on the shoulder, saying that it was the birthright of every upright Bengali to have delusions of grandeur and it came from eating too many fish-heads.

And god forbid, now that she was thinking of taking up writing seriously, would she be expected to TYPE out her articles and all that? She had a poet's hopeless incompatibility with gizmos. She fantasized taking snappy Schumacher type of swerves in the battered family car, but the actual fact was that most of the time she could hardly tell the brake from the clutch. Why, even her basic Arithmetic had stopped evolving after a certain point. It was as if one half of her brain mushrooming all over the place with its super sensitivity to every kind of stimuli and exquisite language skills had, in the process, never really given the other half a chance to develop. As long as the vegetable vendor gave her one kilo or two kilos of the stuff, things were fine. But unexpected things like 750 grams and 900 grams left her totally stumped and speechless. Her lips moved when she shopped. People fell back respectfully, imagining her to be chanting the Krishna mantra so popular at the sunset hour. Only her sons turning away to hide their smirks guessed that Mummy was reciting her multiplication tables.

Sharmila was afraid. The decision to write, taken a few days back was creating a kind of restless turbulence within her. Old thoughts, old angles of perception and old longings were stirring out of long hibernation. Changes were taking place deep within her, like plates of the earth's crust moving menacingly and revealing frightening flashes of magma beneath. What was she going to focus all this suddenly burgeoning energy on, she thought despairingly. Yes, of course, she would write on something close to her heart. Always a little spiritually inclined, she would write about.... "Didi!" screeched her maid shrilly, "the fish man is here." She needed fish urgently. Her brother-in-law, a purely carnivorous gentleman was coming over for dinner that night. Her mind raced as she cleaned the tiny fish. She never left this delicate task to anyone. She loved the pin point accuracy and repetitiveness of slitting fish gills, extricating those nasty things called innards, giving the fish a good wash and piling them up in a silvery mound smelling of sand and sea. The task generally had a soporific effect on her but today her brain was working overtime.

Yes, she would draft an article for the newspaper, she thought pleasurably, about the monolithic Shiv temple back in her hometown. The oldest temple in that region, an architectural marvel with a history that was as interesting as the filigree carvings on it's walls. High stone stairs leading down to the inner sanctum with one row of restless, thirsty minds climbing down single file and another lot of satiated devotees clambering up all day long. Each line of people bent slightly sideways to make way for the other. A cunningly crafted skylight that bathed the Shiv-ling with sunlight in the daytime and sparked it with starlight in the night. And the cold stone Shiv-ling sitting silent for centuries amidst the smell of incense, marigolds and fresh unboiled milk, while the chants of the sadhus echoed back and forth from the stone walls. It was strange how her thoughts which had floated around like aimless asteroids, never straying beyond menus, laundry and Geography projects for years had, at the merest beckoning, come spinning to form the most glorious of configurations. "Ah, Freud pal," she thought, laughing at her own fancies, "you would have liked this bit."

"Shiva," she wrote late into the night in her nightdress, "the easily pleased blue god of destruction, whose generosity is limitless and wrath cosmos-shaking...." The introduction would have to be bombastic since she had no bylines to boast of. Her younger son Bon Bon hung on to her shoulder as she typed, waiting to grab the computer for his interrupted games. What on earth was Mumsy doing at the computer, he thought resentfully, shouldn't she be organising the idli batter for the next day's breakfast or something?

"Didiii!" screeched the maid, "the laundry man is here."

Bon Bon's trousers would have to be given to the laundry. He had got a lapful of cobalt blue colour in Art class the day before. When she got back, Bon Bon was playing a swift Ninja game at the computer. She dislodged him from the chair and attempted to get back to her typing.

"WHERE'S my article?" she howled a second later. "You mean you haven't saved it, Mumsy?" quailed Bon Bon, white-faced. "SAVE it?" screamed Sharmila. "Isn't it bad enough having to type it without having to SAVE the blasted thing?"

The article was finally dispatched (with a lot of fanfare) and peace reigned over the household once more. Sharmila felt curiously elated, weary, quiet and drained all at the same time. Gosh! Trying to be Cinderella and Steinbeck at the same time was no joking matter. Now, a small prayer to the powers above that the editor whose hands it fell into did not suffer from peptic ulcers or have a problem mother-in-law. And then a surreptitious glance into the newspapers everyday to see whether one's byline sparkled in some wonderful corner. A hope that could be fulfilled true and fast or could stretch into days, weeks, months, eternity ... with hope slowly crumbling into despair.

The last weekend of the year was always the most hectic, thought Sharmila. She had, for the umpteenth time, been elected to host the New Year party for the colony kids. Having been elected official cook and entertainer for the colony bash for the last seven years, as in the case of the past years, she had been unable to refuse even this time. Sharmila was born with the inability to say no to any kind of request. According to her cousin Teertha, it was a congenital defect worse than a hole in the heart. Sharmila, by virtue of this trait, stood the undisputed darling of drunkards, eunuchs and lepers who were never turned away disappointed. Her maid walked away with a whopping (and wholly undeserved) bonus during Diwali and bought herself some American diamond jewellery (something Sharmila had never been able to afford for herself). The city came alive to fireworks at midnight. Sharmila lay flopped back on the sofa, all alone amidst scattered balloon ends, torn streamers, empty glasses and plates. She rose tiredly. She'd clean up the party mess first thing tomorrow morning. She'd surf the net for a while now and then crash into bed. God, she felt every bit her forty years at this moment.

"Mumsy!" Bon Bon burst into the room early the next morning. "Your article is in the papers – page one!"

He stopped short. His mother was fast asleep at the computer. Waves of rainbow colour washed over her thin tired face. The monitor after a long, patient wait had given up on her. The gray harshness of the screen had given way to a sparkling, multi-hued screen saver, and to the eleven-year-old Bon Bon, it seemed as if a million stars were exploding.

OF BIRD SONG

Supriya had a thing about mynahs. Those chocolate-brown birds with chrome-yellow beaks and eye liner and the flash of dazzling white as they took wing. They could either make or break her day. At the age of thirty-five, her heart still leapt with illogical joy when she saw two mynahs, while the sight of a lone bird made her feel jittery the whole day long. The twins Dinky and Tinky could be heard chanting, "One for sorrow, two for joy, three for letter, four for boy..." all evening as they played with their colony friends. Her friend Malaika, on seeing her panic-stricken expression at seeing a solo mynah would invariably burst out laughing, urging her to look around for the mate who was bound to be around somewhere close. But Supriya would hurry back home, forgetting to wave out to her friend Bubla and anticipating floods, fire, cyclones, bomb blasts, absent maid servants, anything.

The growing years for Supriya had been difficult ones. She was the second of the three children and had missed out on substantial parental pampering for being just that – a middle child. Her elder brother (like most Bengali eldest brothers) was God incarnate and the mother's pet. His wishes were laws, his lunch menus a matter of national importance and his study hour sacred. Her youngest sibling was fair, plump and pretty, the baby of the family and her father's pet. Supriya grew up without really belonging to any specific camp. She was thin, dark and plain. And everybody made it a point to remind her that she was thin, dark and plain. Her mother followed it up by saying never mind, she had the family's brains. Her brother followed it up by recommending multi-vitamin capsules. Her father did not say much but on her 18th birthday, he gifted her membership to a gym named "Bright and Beautiful." Supriya grew up lusting for a glowing complexion, bright eyes and lustrous hair.

With the coming of adolescence, Supriya felt a great urge to talk. There was this awesome, chronic need to unburden herself to people. Everybody from maids and neighbours to total strangers had to listen to her cathartic conversation from time to time. She once frightened her seventy-year-old grocer by explaining in graphic detail the hormonal changes that had come over her after the birth of her twins. And how her bustline, after breast-feeding her twins for years, had gone up to a horrifying 46 inches. The grocer had fled, never to step into her house again. Supriya often wondered why he sent the flour and the sugar with these blank-faced delivery boys sporting painted nails and single earrings and never came himself.

Supriya's mother-in-law lived with her. As a teenager, Trupti Banerjee had been forced to leave her green, pond-filled, paddy-waving hometown in Dhaka, East Bengal and migrate to India during the Partition. She never got tired of relating the Partition horror stories to anyone who happened to cross her path, even fifty odd years after the event. Arguing endlessly with her husband over matters ranging from cricket to fish took up most of Trupti Banerjee's time and energy. But the sudden demise of Mr. Banerjee put an end to this pleasurable activity.

Widowed with unexpected suddenness, Mrs. Banerjee Senior (as she was popularly called) decided to make a career out of her various ailments. With the hypochondriac's luxurious sense of gloating, she took to regaling her son and daughter-in-law every morning with the pattern of her nightly insomnia and the intricacies of her bowel movement. Her son Shubhojeet, as a result, came home every evening laden with bags of spinach. Constipation, he wisely guessed, led to some of the worst mother-in-law daughter-in-law tiffs. Her grand daughters Dinky and Tinky could be heard telling their friends, "Thamma looks like Olive but eats like Popeye!" Trupti could never comprehend why the little girls burst into giggles every time she entered the room.

Trupti Banerjee did not treasure particularly fond memories of her late husband. She never forgave him for remaining a mere Central Government employee all his life and for the family having to live in the dreary, lime-washed, stone-floored government quarters. Above all, she never forgave him for being shorter than her. Only the Partition crisis (and her being a nubile girl at the time) had forced her to marry such a runt, she was fond of telling people. In happier circumstances she could have had the tallest and finest of grooms!

When Supriya first entered the Banerjee household as a young bride, her mother-in-law had bristled with apprehension and resentment. Would this chit of a girl contest her position as Queen of Constipation and Insomnia? But the hale and hearty Supriya, with boundless energy and a healthy quota of ten hours sleep had quickly put her fears to rest. Supriya, thus endearing herself to her mother-in-law by the virtues of good health, settled down companionably every afternoon to listen to the Tales of Partition....

Enough is enough, thought the high-spirited Supriya when the twins turned seven, it is time I did something concrete with my life. Being a homemaker for life was not her idea of bliss. She remembered with nostalgia her brief stint as a working girl before marriage. Writing copy for inane advertisements throughout the day and rattling back home in a second class compartment at the sunset hour. Clattering past dingy houses at touching distance. Slicing past shabby kitchens with gleaming pots, tired-looking men in striped underwear, little children with bare bottoms squatting inches away from the thundering trains – a neat cross section of the city squalor that the sunset lit up with such tender vitality.

What career plans could she start with now? She had accompanied her friend (an Avon representative) once to one of her meetings with a customer. She remembered sitting in a strange, lovely drawing room in the silences of mid-morning. Coffee smells wafted from the kitchen while her friend laid out a fascinating array of jars and bottles. Sunlight filtered through the liquid gold of skin serums, the amber depths of perfumes and the cool blues of colognes. Talk was all about that magical, elusive thing called beauty. But, thought Supriya, declining the dealership a few days later, you would have to be terribly well groomed at all times for such things and she could barely stop herself from looking like a shipwreck at the best of times.

Shubhojeet watched his wife's mercurial mood changes stoically. Every individual (he had this private little theory) was born with a certain quota of emotional energy. In Supriya's case, the quota was so high that it went spilling all over the place.

"Why don't you try your hand at scriptwriting? Your postgraduation in English might come useful," he suggested mildly.

Yeah, thought Supriya, not a bad idea. After all, didn't she have enough real life drama to draw from? The recent happenings at her elder brother's house were a case in point. Boudi had stalked out of the house claiming that she had caught Dada pinching the maid. Dada, on the other hand, condemned Boudi for making eyes at the television actor who lived across. Wonderfully stimulating fireworks had followed through the whole weekend, with the entire family having to choose sides. Yah, she'd write feisty stuff that would make the audiences sit up and forget the popcorn. No subtle stuff for her please. She'd rather leave that to the likes of Mrinal Sen and Satyajit Ray. Why, you never knew when their movies got over till people came treading all over your corns in their hurry to get to the exit. She couldn't be a scribe – too much effort remembering ministers' names. Besides, her reading habits had deteriorated to reading mere bills and bank statements.

Bubla left early in the morning on her first day as scriptwriter. Mrs. Banerjee, her mouth stained red with betel-leaf juice, murmured a little prayer for her daughter-in-law. Under the traditionally wrapped white cotton sari jingling with keys beat a staunchly feminist heart. With heartfelt sincerity she wanted her daughter-in-law to succeed in her new career. She had a huge array of gods, goddesses and saints, framed and garlanded, in one corner of her bedroom. Separated by six inches of wall were exquisite prints of contemporary Indian artists (Mrs. Banerjee understood and revered Art though personally lacking in artistic skills). The paintings were at a slightly lower level than the gods, almost as if to gently remind the viewer that though exalted in their own field, they were in no way to be confused with divinity.

On the first Sunday of September Supriya got hit by a solid rubber ball minutes after she saw a single mynah.

"Aunty! Ball please!" a six-footer held out his hand grinning cheekily. Supriya hurled the ball back, grim-faced.

"I wish these hulks would not call me Aunty. It makes me feel as old as a mummy," she grumbled irately to the twins walking alongside.

"But you are a Mummy, our Mummy," Dinky said, confused.

"Oh, the sarcophagus one," explained Supriya.

"The sarco-wazzat?" chimed in Tinky.

"Oh, forget it!" snapped Supriya, busy with her own dark thoughts. Everything that could go wrong was going wrong these days. A solo mynah early in the morning, a ball on the head minutes later, and towering hunks calling her Aunty! Could things get worse? And last night! The horror of seeing her name in the credits at the end of the soap (for which she wrote the script) as "Assistant Conceptualizer" after being the sole brain behind the serial all these days. And Vinita, curse the woman, had the cheek to appoint herself Chief Conceptualizer just because she happened to be the producer. Why, the whole idea of the heroine losing her memory on the death of her husband, regaining it in snatches and having her childhood sweetheart walk in at the opportune moment was entirely hers, the copyright of Supriya Banerjee! That scheming cat Vinita, stealing her ideas and trying to cut her out of things!

In the last six months, Supriya had come to the conclusion that she was one of those people destined to be permanently unestablished. She would always be an insecure beginner, struggling to prove herself against suave, sophisticated veterans who had cut their milk teeth under the studio lights. But she was damned if she was going to take Shubhojeet's advice and resign.

With the new Feng Shui classes, mirrors vanished from the house. Shubhojeet missed them. With a balding man's masochistic need to keep viewing the scene of tragedy, he would peek at his rear view in the strategically placed mirrors from time to time. Was the new wonder hair potion working or was his head going from a daisy to a sunflower? Now of course, there were no mirrors to check out in. Supriya, in her zeal for her new vocation banished mirrors, but liberally planted bamboo shoots, crystals and artificial waterfalls all over the living room. The latest addition was a glass tank full of lively turtles (said to attract wealth and prosperity by the Feng Shui master). Shubhojeet would dart glances of pure hatred at the turtles in moments of solitude, but Supriya was too caught up in the new excitement to notice. The main door would have to be shifted a little to the left, she told Shubhojeet, and the bathroom a little more to the right. The kitchen platform was all wrong and something would have to be done about it. The bedroom door should ideally face North for good energy flow, she continued animatedly, and if possible the entire building should hop a couple of steps backwards. Shubhojeet started staying late in office.

Supriya slept late into Sunday morning – one of the few days she got to sleep late. She got up to find a minor commotion on in the kitchen. One of the turtles had been squished underfoot. No one was ready to own up. Saturday nights were night-outs for the turtles. One of them had not made it to Sunday morning.

Supriya was livid. She could see her second career option getting squashed like the turtle. Supriya always felt a kind of madness around the month of October. The smell of hot sun on tall grass after months of gray rain always sent her spirits into a kind of mad, intoxicated spin. Her family would look at her strangely at such times. Dinky and Tinky were leaving on a school trip a few days later and Shubhojeet was taking his mother to Kolkata for the usual annual sibling fete. She would visit her school friend Sujata for a week, she decided. Anyways, she was career-less at the moment after Turtle Death. She would recharge her batteries at Sujata's place. She did not know it then, but it would be a week that would stay etched in her mind forever.

The very Tamilian Sujata was a complete contrast to the flamboyant Supriya. She had long hair which she wore plaited and which she regularly oiled with coconut oil, and on her forehead were half a dozen dots and dashes of religious connotations. She firmly believed in wearing nightgowns of indeterminate colours all day long. On rare occasions when she had to go shopping, she wrapped herself tightly in an inconspicuous looking synthetic sari, successfully hiding her femininity from the world and herself. When she passed by, one got a whiff of incense, sandalwood and temples on high windy mountains. Safety pins hung from her bangles. Timing was everything. She entered her house and embarked on journeys at auspicious, precisely timed moments.

The meeting of the two friends was noisy. Supriya hugged her friend so tight that Sujata burped. She then went cathartic with a vengeance while Sujata supplied the idlis, the appams and the sympathy. Really, she thought, life was tough on poor Supriya!

Sujata's husband Jairaj was a quiet man. He went about his business quietly, leaving the two friends to each other.

After lunch he left home for a long quiet walk. Returning some time later with a gray face, he flopped onto the living room sofa complaining of a chest pain. By the time a panic-stricken Sujata had run to phone the family doctor, Jairaj C. had turned on his side and died wordlessly, apology written all over his face. And Supriya saw her calm, god-fearing friend of a million pujas fall apart into pieces.

The days that followed were a collage of nightmares for the two women. The silence after the initial wailing, the icy marigold wreaths and the numbing chants of the priests seemed interminable. Supriya suddenly found herself relegated to the role of protector and listener – the supporting actress as it were. It was a new role for someone who was used to being centre stage at all times. It took three and a half days of exhaustive brainwashing on Supriya's part to convince Sujata into declining the hefty compensation offered by her husband's office and demand a job instead. A long dusty search in aluminium trunks pushed under beds yielded Sujata's dog-eared graduation certificates. On day nine, Supriya succeeded in helping Sujata put together pieces of herself and convinced her that there was life beyond rasam, rice and spouse.

Supriya trudged home wearily, her overnight bag weighing heavily on her shoulders. Was the person she was last Monday and the person she was today truly one and the same? She seemed to have travelled an entirely new dimension in these last ten days. It took a tragedy at uncomfortably close quarters to click one's perspective into position, she thought. When she left, Sujata had stood waving at the balcony, a forlorn figure in a washed out nightgown.

The house gleamed, spick and span and silent as she unlatched the door. Her maid had been working hard in her absence it appeared. The twins and her husband were due back home the next day. She'd bake a chocolate cake for them, she thought happily as she showered, and perhaps try her hand at some Chinese cooking. She felt a surge of contentment as she lay down on the bed. They would all be romping on this queen-sized bed in a day's time, limbs and hair entangled as they always did on family reunions. Supriya felt deliriously sleepy. A garishly painted face of Swami Vivekananda gazed back at her from a calendar (her mother-in-law believed in planting a Bengali calendar crowded with saints and freedom fighters in every room). Below the face, in terrible calligraphy were some lines:

> *You are the path, you are the destination*
> *You are the question, also the answer*
> *You are truth, you are illusion*
> *You are infinite yet void*
> *Do not go around searching for meaning, O friend*
> *All the wonders you look for are within yourself.*

Now which goofball, thought Supriya, grinning to herself, had thought of that one? Must be the calendar-maker's own little contribution, she thought drowsily. Sleep was fast overtaking her. It had taken her fourteen years to realize that if one looked hard enough there always was a second mynah. Must remember to tell that to Malaika.

A SUITABLE DEATH

Doctor Tripathi called on the Sharmas when the family was at breakfast. Breakfast was generally a hearty affair in the Sharma household. Today's menu was ghee-soaked parathas to which each person added an extra dollop of butter, and tall glasses of lassi topped with thick cream. Did these people even know how to spell "cholesterol?" wondered Dr. Tripathi sourly. He cleared his throat. Now came the tricky part.... "The report came into my clinic just a while ago," he said in a kind of rush. "Malignancy is confirmed. I'm sorry."

Three sets of shocked faces looked up at him. Mr. Sharma's mouth hung open in shock showing half-chewed food and Dr. Tripathi hastily looked away. Mrs. Harpreet Sharma and her daughter Sweety wore looks of stunned disbelief. Sharma Dadi who had just been about to enter the room, heard all. ~

She stood transfixed. Cancer! She had cancer! Why, such things happened only to people in the movies! Or to other people! And she, Wahe guru, was only seventy-two! Raised voices could be heard in the dining area as a clamour of questions rose around the Doctor. Unnoticed by the others, she turned on her heel and walked away to her room, her mind in turmoil. Once inside, she walked straight up to the dressing table mirror. The reflection showed a woman with cheeks ruddy with a high fat diet (and possible high blood pressure), an upright posture, a proud 48-inch bustline and hips to match. What a pity that one had to get marching orders just when one was looking one's best, thought Dadi. Damn, blast and curse the wretched doctor. Couldn't he have organized for her to live a couple more years? At least till Sweety got married?

She pulled shut the window curtains and lay down on the bed feeling unusually contemplative. Her life on the whole had not been too bad, she thought, excepting for her husband's death a few years back. But maybe ... maybe it was getting to be pack up time after all...? Hadn't things been changing slowly and subtly of late? Her usually attentive son got a rather glazed, unseeing look on his face these days when she grumbled about her arthritic knee. Her favourite granddaughter Sweety had taken to talking to her in a deafening volume (did she think she was deaf ... well, maybe she was, just a little) and chased her with deodorants all day long. Sweety's friends laughed uproariously whenever she entered the room and she often felt like an escaped inmate of a loony bin. Her grandson had long clubbed her with the fossils of the Paleolithic Age on which subject he was making a school chart, and the less said about the servants the better. Have I outlived my welcome, wondered Sharma Dadi.

"One month," she had heard Dr. Tripathi say in answer to the cacophony of questions. "I'd give her roughly one month."

Well, if she had to go, she had to go, thought Dadi sportingly. But she'd live it up in this one month. She would see every adult horny movie in town, she would meet all her relatives (whom she hated privately), eat at every fancy restaurant and buy a dozen designer salwar-kameezes (which could later go to Harpreet). Now, what would be a memorable way to die? Maybe like those old Hollywood heroines who died in languid grace, every curl in place, with a slim cigarette dangling from a limp, gloved hand? She smoked bidis on the sly but that may not look equally attractive on her death bed. Or maybe she could die on a wave of impressive dialogue delivery like the Hindi film heroes? No, no. She may not have the necessary stamina or the respiratory abilities for that. She pleasurably visualized herself surrounded by grieving and repentant friends and family. Serve the idiots right for neglecting her lately. They would be seeped in guilt. She would have to look well-groomed in her last moments, remember to keep her mouth shut while dying.... An attractive dead woman was so much more appealing than an ugly one, she thought. Yes, maybe in a fortnight's time, in anticipation of the coming event, she would get one of those new-fangled facials where they used pure gold to revive aging skin. A manicure might be in order. A pedicure wasn't necessary as the feet would be inside the shroud and why waste money? Maybe, for the first time in her life, she'd get her arms waxed (that cat Rekha Guha downstairs would be waiting to say something spiteful, her favourite topic being Punjabi women and hirsutism). She hadn't planned so much in years, not even for Harish's wedding. Really, dying seemed to be an exciting business after all....

Harish Sharma sat motionless in his dining chair for a long time. Life without Mummyji! Unthinkable! Why, she was like the Gateway of India or the Red Fort. One did not expect such things to just vanish! Mothers were not supposed to ditch one and vamoose just like that. Who would make his favourite radish parathas and the unforgettable dal makhani? Those wonderful recipes would perish with her....

Harish Sharma was considered something of an oddity, not just by his friends but also by his family. Laidback and dreamy, he took life as it came. He could never understand that class of people whose mission it was to gallop to the finishing line as fast as possible. The lean, leashed hungry feeling of wanting a thing very badly and not being able to reach it was the kind of poetic emotion Harish revelled in and he hated achieving any kind of personal goal, no matter how small. It gave him a flat, empty kind of feeling, rather like the post-prandial symptoms discussed so widely in women's magazines (Harish regularly read woman's magazines). What was the use of burning up the achievement track in a tearing hurry, he was fond of asking his wife Harpreet, and what was one to do after that? Sit and play solitaire? It was another matter that Harish hardly had any goals to speak of. He had inherited his father's flourishing business that dealt in automobile spare parts and he was at liberty to sit back and dream his life away. Fantasies were so much more satisfying than reality, besides. They did not involve body odour, flatulence and ill-fitting underwear, small things that often spoilt life's grander moments. His dreams were sculpted along lofty lines and in them he was judge and jury, chairman and director, cricketer and matinee idol all rolled into one. His wife Harpreet, in a rare moment of insight realized that her husband had stopped evolving beyond the age of twelve.

Harish wrote poems. To his mother's utter disgust. After penning down his verses, Harish read them through with meticulous care and was generally amazed at his own eloquence and talent. It was another matter that the poems all came back with the editor's regrets whenever he attempted to get them published. But he continued sprouting poetry unfazed.

"Nice man," said women of Harish, feeling quite safe in his company, "but not quite there."

Now this sudden bit of news had got him all unnerved. Mummyji's passing would be akin to the World Trade Center collapsing. Of course, the medical bills would get lighter. He spent a few thousands every year on Mummyji's blood pressure pills, Calcium supplements, diuretics, vitamins ... God, would he have to perform the last rites? How awful! He had an aversion towards religious rituals of any kind. And how would they take the body down seven flights of steps? The staircase had such cramped corners. These builders never thought of such important details while making buildings. Besides, the lift was also too small to accommodate a supine body. He would have to tip the watchmen heavily and keep them happy. Mummyji weighed a good eighty kilograms. He was going to need a lot of help on that particular day.

Harpreet finished clearing up the breakfast table and slowly trudged to her bedroom. The morning's happenings had knocked her out completely. This was the time she generally read the Sunday papers for a while. She read the Sunday papers all the way till next Sunday. She loved reading the Sunday papers. A yoga teacher who told you how to get that tummy in, a shrink who told you how to get your brains fixed, a socialite who told you how to get your table manners right, and a recipe page that undid your tummy, your mind and your manners. So that you could start all over again with next Sunday's papers....

Harpreet had spent her childhood in Kolkata. Soft-spoken, feminine and with Bengali cultural influences running strong within her, she believed in cool cotton wear and soft soul music. On entering the Sharma household as a young bride, she had gone into a state of culture shock that lasted an entire year.

"Can you give Vivek a massage?" her mother-in-law had asked her a day after her marriage, startling her considerably.

Harpreet had been covered in confusion. She was a broad-minded, convent-educated girl but give her strapping young brother-in-law a MASSAGE? It took her a while to understand matters and get the entire business of pronunciations sorted out. The young Vivek had to be periodically given "messages," it seemed, and "mayor" and "player" often meant "measure" and "pleasure." Her mother-in-law, with her rambunctious taste in music, gizmos and nylon garments had filled her with a nameless horror initially. Till she realized that under the crude bluster and layers of polyester clothing was a warm, big-hearted woman with an infinite capacity to laugh at herself. She started attending Saturday evening satsangs with Mummyji (where Mummyji was chief dholak player). Mummyji, on these occasions beat a dholak with a steel spoon with unbridled gusto while her friends sang themselves hoarse. Everybody wore white. Harpreet, after the initial shock and momentary deafness joined in with gusto. On the basis of the weekly satsangs, a comfortable equation sprung up between the two women, which lasted over the years. This morning's happenings had shocked Harpreet beyond words. Life without her feisty mother-in-law? Unthinkable! And more than any blood relative, it was Harpreet who grieved....

Sweety stood on the balcony, stunned and teary-eyed with the quick sincere grief of the young. Later on her thoughts would crawl into forbidden and traitorous paths heralding the end of childhood. Life without Dadi! Why, her long lustrous hair, the envy of all her friends was entirely the outcome of Dadi's regular oiling. And every time her parents had acted stuffy about her long line of boyfriends, Dadi had stepped in championing her cause. What were a few boyfriends, she was fond of telling her parents contemptuously, mere accessories in a girl's life and not an issue at all!

The time Vicky had come home had been quite embarrassing though. To get Vicky with his awesome top-of-the-class IQ to visit her home was a feat in itself. None of her classmates had been able to manage the impossible to date. The entrance of her house as she came home with her gaggle of friends and Vicky had been littered with Dadi's special winter pickles and papads catching the morning sun. Her friends had tiptoed gingerly over the line of fragile obstacles and thrown themselves into the nearest pieces of furniture. When everybody had settled down to tea and conversation, Dadi had stomped into the house arthritically, her hip held out at an angle of forty-five degrees. She had hobbled up to Vicky and stationed herself at nose-to-nose distance. Suddenly, she had jabbed him in the ribs with a stubby, pickle-smelling finger, taking him totally unawares and knocking him down into the sofa.

"Doesn't your mother give you almond milk every night?" she had asked the shell-shocked Vicky, "Why are those ribs sticking out so?"

There was a moment of sickening silence till Sweety's friend Sheila saved the situation by bursting into noisy giggles. Vicky had managed a watery smile before the awkwardness of the moment passed and general conversation set in. Dadi had not cared much for Vicky. Too full of himself for one thing and too little body hair for another. Eyes too small in size and set too close together and absolutely no sense of fun. Not son-in-law material at all!

"Now, look at that gem of a boy Khokon Guha...." Dadi was perpetually telling Sweety.

Sweety had on many occasions tried to tackle the delicate business of waxing and deodorants with Dadi.

"You can't go around with a handlebar moustache, Dadi! And the hairs on your arms prick me like needles when you hug me. Besides, you can't wear nylons all day long without using a deodorant," Sweety had protested strongly.

"Nonsense!" Dadi had exploded. "There is no need to camouflage the smell of sweat and true hard work. And only miserable, poverty-stricken unfortunates wear cotton! And what is a little body hair? Such a lovely natural thing in a woman!"

With Dadi gone, the drawing room would no longer be an obstacle race, thought Sweety. No pickles and papads at unexpected corners waiting to trip one up. No one would throw the miserable Khokon Guha at her head anymore and no more fear of Dadi breaking wind deafeningly before her friends. She would have a room to herself and life would change dramatically....

Doctor Tripathi called on the Sharmas when they were at breakfast again. Breakfast was bread pakoras accompanied by apple milkshake. The doctor cleared his throat nervously a couple of times, avoiding direct eye contact with anybody in particular.

"There has been an unpardonable mistake," he croaked out finally. "The medical reports had got mixed up. Mrs. Sharma's growth is benign. With a little bit of medication she should be fine."

He fled.

The Sharma household has been strangely silent since then.

MIRROR IMAGE

Bubla Bose sat in her usual chair in the balcony, holding an old mouldy diary in her hands. Thank God her mother was not around. She would have flung the mouldy diary as far as she could (Mould! The worst thing for asthma, Bubla!). Years back when she was a child, a distant aunt whom she remembered addressing as "Nirja Pishi" had come to live with them for some time. She must not have been particularly fond of children for Bubla had no special memories of her. She only remembered a pencil slim woman, all teeth, flitting around the house silently, smelling of musk. And like her, an asthmatic. That was all.

Curious about her after all these years, Bubla's questions about her whereabouts were met with frigid silence from her mother and a hunted, uneasy evasion from her father. Some days later, while searching for an album in the store room, Bubla had come across a moth-eaten diary neatly inscribed with the owner's name, "NIRJA BOSE." With swift cunning she had tucked it into her baggy T-shirt and smuggled it to her room. She had to wait three whole days for an hour of privacy to read it. Her parents were setting off this afternoon for their monthly dental checkup and this was the hour of the detective.

Bubla flipped open the diary. The first few pages were disappointingly empty. Writing started on the seventh page – frenzied, hurried writing. Bubla read avidly with a growing sense of strange uneasy deja vu:

Naina came into my life when I was ten. She appeared seemingly out of nowhere when I was on my way to school. The morning for me had been particularly bad. Granny was in the sourest of moods and I seemed to be doing all the wrong things. Setting out for school was a blessed relief. The road to school wound through a wooded stretch and there she was suddenly, grinning at me from ear to ear as if she had known me all her life. More or less the same age as me but man, was she pretty! Introductions over, she fell into step besides me and walked me all the way to school. How come she wasn't in class and which school was she in anyway, I asked at the school gate. But she just smiled and vanished round the corner.

My parents died when I was five. My mother had been petite, graceful and tact personified – everything a woman should be. I was gaunt, buck-toothed and gauche – everything a girl should not be. If anyone had to drop the crystal at a party, it had to be me. If anyone had to contract chickenpox a day before the family wedding, it had to be me.

"Oh! Nirja!" people were perpetually groaning in despair. I seemed to have a jinx on me from the very onset of my life.

With the death of my parents my life changed completely. My grandmother was furious at losing a slavish son and a docile daughter-in-law whom she could steamroller at will. And to top it all she was landed with an unattractive and unmanageable granddaughter. Not only was I plain looking and brutally frank, but I was also perpetually hungry – probably the biggest irritant of them all. She had to feed me well as even the loss of half a kilogram of weight was noticed and commented upon by the neighbours. Eventually, Gran realized that it was impossible for her to cope with my growing appetite and Pushpa moved in. She was wizened, jet black and a whiz cook. We were an uneasy three-female household. Pushpa did not speak much. She chewed tobacco and watched. Watched faces, watched moods, watched words spat out, watched nuances hiding furtively behind the words, watched seasons change and winter leaves flutter down year after year, all in sphinx-like silence. She watched me stumble out of a difficult childhood and into a tumultuous adolescence.

I had declared war with the whole world. I did not have adoring parents, hi-fi vacations, lavish birthday parties, the lot. But I had a sarcastic tongue that could cut anyone to size. It was my policy to be rude to one and all. But beneath it all I was a confused coward. And dowdy besides. I was afraid to experiment with clothes and hair, afraid to go to a dentist and get braces for my teeth. With boys around I turned gawky and unsure. I lived in a twilit world of rage, hate and despair.

But I must say this of Naina – she was always there to cheer me up even when I was at my lowest and most uncommunicative. I admired her tremendously. She was pretty, had a flair for clothes and small pearly teeth. The last in my opinion was the most enviable of attributes. I shall never forget that windy Wednesday when it all started. We were walking through the woods in companionable silence. I had had a massive row with Gran early in the morning and it was a blessed relief to be out of the house. Naina suddenly bent and plucked a sprig of foxgloves which were in bloom all over the hills. She held the stem in her hand and gently caressed her cheek with the blooms, smiling at me all the while.

"Foxgloves have such immense possibilities, don't they, Nirja?" she asked me slyly.

Foxgloves? Those silly mauve bell-like flowers? I told her as much.

"Oh, Nirja! Don't you pay attention to your Agatha Christie favourites? A couple of foxglove leaves is all you need to send someone..." she looked skywards eloquently. Up? Up where? What on earth was she talking about? Suddenly, my dim memory seemed to stir. A few foxglove leaves mixed in a person's food, I had read somewhere, and the person eating it was sure to drift into an endless siesta of death ... I stood transfixed.

"Whom do you mean?" I asked fearfully.

"The house is legally yours, Nirja. Imagine the freedom of

living in it all on your own. The thorn in your side can be easily got rid of ... Gran...."

I raced away without bothering to answer her. My head was exploding with strange new emotions. I was in bed with a severe headache that whole afternoon.

Pushpa had started goofing up and that was rather convenient for me. She put sugar instead of saccharine in Gran's early morning tea and poppy seeds in the French bean dish for lunch. Eating poppy seeds was sacrilege in Gran's eyes and she hated the stuff with both her taste buds and her morals. In her opinion, poppy seeds made one drowsy, were addictive, and having it was as much an offense as taking opium openly. She blasted Pushpa for being a senile, inefficient hag who deserved to be put into the Old Folks' Home. Pushpa chewed tobacco and remained unperturbed. I suspected that a major factor in her equanimity was partial and selective deafness.

The whole operation was childishly simple. A plateful of chopped spinach lay on the kitchen platform waiting to be cooked. Pushpa had gone to answer Gran's bedroom summons. I casually dropped the chopped foxglove leaves into the spinach pile and clambered out of the kitchen window. Naina was waiting for me. I was supposed to be in school at this hour and I'm sure no one had seen me steal back into the house. I detested spinach and Pushpa did not touch the stuff, saying it got caught in her dentures. All undue complications were out of the way. That was that.

Gran was cremated with a lot of fanfare with practically the whole population of the tiny town of Sonarpur attending.

She had been the oldest and the most hated resident of Sonarpur and people turned out in big numbers to watch her go. Pushpa was half-heartedly berated by everybody for being sloppy, bird-brained and blind as a bat as well. Imagine not noticing the difference between the two kinds of leaves! Honestly, the woman needed soda-glasses for sure!

Life was a dream come true for some time. Go to bed as late as one pleased and no limitations on the quantity of black coffee consumed. The volume of music did not have to be funereally low and cigarettes did not have to be kept hidden anymore. Life was a ball. Naina was a permanent fixture around the place. Strangely, Pushpa never offered tea, coffee or snacks to Naina.

She always came with just one plate or a single steaming cup for me. Not that Naina minded. She never ate or drank at my place. Pushpa had started watching me. In her eyes was a secret – my secret. It made me uneasy. How much did she know, how much did she guess? As usual, Naina my friend, guide and mentor came to the rescue. "If one old fogey can be got rid of, why not another?" she asked.

The lonely path from Pushpa's ramshackle hut to our house skirted a pond, murky and deep. Pushpa, stiff with age and arthritis and devoid of swimming skills would be easy game. Early one morning, I stood hidden behind a neem tree, Naina beside me. I heard Pushpa's grunts as she laboured down the path. It was ridiculously easy. A gentle push and she was sliding down rapidly towards the water. She barely managed a croak before she went under.

We stood respectfully till the bubbles in the water

subsided. All around us was an eerie silence. We walked home in silence. Naina had promised to teach me to cook.

It never struck me that some early riser walking through the woods could have witnessed the whole thing. They came to take me the next day. The audacity! A couple of men and a woman who held my arm in a grip of steel. Was I being arrested? Would I have to see Pushpa's bloated body at the police station? Where was Naina? Never had I needed her so badly.

But they did not take me to the police station. It was a place all in white. A white bed in a white room and the all-pervading smell of antiseptic and fear. A typical hospital smell. A man in white arrived and started asking me soft-voiced questions. But I was not going to answer, no way! I had seen enough movies to know that my statements could be used cunningly against me. I sat like a female Buddha – silent and immobile. A few other men in white came and stood near the door. My interrogator got up and joined them. There was a hushed round of conversation between them.

"Schizophrenia," I heard one of them mutter. "Multiple personality disorder...."

They went away, leaving me alone. I dropped a glass and watched it shatter with a feeling of satisfaction. I wasn't going to be an easy patient, I decided rebelliously. I'll teach those smug stupid men in white a lesson.

Schizowazzat....? What was the term they used?

I went to the mirror and stared. The mirror seemed to swim before my eyes. Naina stared back at me. What was happening? I started to laugh hysterically. Naina also laughed uproariously. I stopped laughing. And Naina stopped laughing. I rushed to smash the mirror with my fists. The girl in the mirror rushed back at me. The contorted face that stared back at me was, oh my god, Nirja ... Naina ... Nirja ... Naina ... Naina....

THE PILGRIM

When Teertha Chakravarty scrambled out of the taxi at the airport, she realised that she was wearing mismatched earrings. She grabbed a trolley, shoved her luggage onto it and marched to the check in counter feeling giggly, vague and happy. Travelling always made her feel like this. She hadn't had time to get herself a much-needed haircut, her nails needed filing and she was wearing mismatched earrings, but she felt on top of the world. Flying was always such a lovely experience – imprisoned in the confines of an aircraft with (hopefully) silent strangers, cruising into sunsets and soaking in the feeling of timelessness....

Teertha slept on the flight, a coma-like deep stupor common to the sleep deprived. Her mouth hung slightly open, giving her gamine pixie face a slightly surprised look. Sudden screams and commotion jolted her out of her slumber. People all around her were shouting, screaming, scampering and holding on to one another as the aircraft swayed from side to side sickeningly. The stewardesses seemed to have given up all attempts at being bravely professional and were sobbing on each other's shoulders. God help me, thought Teertha in amazement, brushing sleep out of her eyes, we are crashing! She half stood up and sank back again into her seat. There was nothing one could do really. You either had hysterics or calmly watched death approach. Strange how mixed up her emotions were at this moment. She had never been enamoured with this whole mediocre business of living, an unavoidable situation that was thrust upon one, and you really had no say in the matter. She always wondered why the detection of a terminal disease sent the hero or heroine into a tizzy of grief in the movies. Had any doctor told her that she was going to die shortly, she would have hugged him tightly till he burped. But all that was theoretical. Now that death was actually rushing up at her at the speed of a hundred miles an hour, why did she have to remember cozy things like hot coffee in the rain and retro songs on sleepless nights? And to die like this, mentally unprepared, in violence and wearing mismatched earrings...? There was an ear-splitting scrunch, a blinding flash, pain and then darkness....

Teertha opened her eyes to birdsong. A filigree of deep green leaves blotted out the sky. Little kerchief-sized patches of blue were visible among the branches of trees. She moved her limbs gingerly. Yah, all her faculties and limbs seemed intact. But she had bruises all over, big purple patches of frozen blood. She lay back on the grass and looked all around. There was complete silence. Silence so heavy that its weight seemed almost oppressive. Why, thought Teertha in wonder, even her thoughts sounded vulgarly loud. Gossamer cobwebs hung between branches, catching the sunset and droplets of evening dew. Where on earth was she and where were the other passengers from the aircraft? Night would be falling soon, though she would rather not think about that now. She stood up slowly, trying to regain her equilibrium. As she started walking, her trudging steps with dry leaves crackling underfoot seemed deafeningly loud.

Every path drew a blank. A blue-green twilight was overtaking the forest and Teertha's skin prickled with cold and fear. Never in her entire life had she felt so alone. Well, she thought, trying to inject some humour into the situation, she would no longer have to school her face into an expression of polite interest for people around. Her eyes could now unfocus and her face slacken into a vacant expression in this wilderness. But fear clogged her every step. Where would she spend the night? The evening star was beginning to twinkle high up beyond the trees. Would humans find her before any wild animals did?

Suddenly she spotted a figure in the half-light. "Hey!" screamed Teertha, "Hey, wait!"

But the figure just walked faster, impervious to her cries. She ran on, stumbling and falling but was unable to catch the nebulous figure. And almost as suddenly as it had appeared, the figure vanished into the undergrowth. Teertha stopped short, breathless. There was something in the woods in front of her, a big dark opaque structure darker than the darkness around. They were ruins! Broken staircases, chipped carvings and crumbling railings belonging to a mansion with the eerie grandeur of some forgotten era. But the inside, Teertha discovered on investigation, was wonderfully dry and smelt fresh. Thank god (and also the strange figure that had led her to the ruins), at least she now had a warm place to sleep in. She dropped down into a corner exhausted and her eyes closed before she had even finished her thoughts.

When she woke up, a man was sitting on a boulder a few feet away from her, watching her. The first things she noticed about him were his eyes. Strange inward looking eyes with the sheen of mirrors. Looking into them, she got the uncanny feeling of seeing herself not as she liked to see herself but as she really was. His age seemed indeterminate and could have been anything from forty to seventy years.

"Ha! You're awake!" he sounded relieved. "Do you think you could get up?" She rose gingerly, shaking all the while like a newborn foal. "You'll need a wash," he sounded brisk and practical. "Come!" She followed him down a narrow path. Thick undergrowth closed in on them, branches of trees brushing their faces, hair and limbs like green ghostly fingers. They came upon a sparkling spring of fresh water which gushed down a hill to form a clear little pool. The man stretched out a hand towards the water and vanished into the trees.

Teertha drank water thirstily like a greedy child. She then splashed herself all over. The bruises felt blissfully cool after the splashing. She waded in the sunlit water, wet clothes clinging to her person, and stared into their crystal depths. The reflection that stared back at her was disturbing. Her hair spilled all over her shoulders in wild abandon, a rip at the shoulder of her T-shirt showed skin, and her whole person appeared wet, wild and wanton. She kept her disturbed eyes hidden as the stranger reappeared. He seemed to smile though not a muscle of his face moved. He sat down on a rock and looked at her with eyes that seemed to read her mind like a book. "The seer sees no colour, no gender, no age. He merely sees the labyrinths of the mind. Just as true vision is not bound by time and space but sees the past, present and the future as one linear totality," he said softly. Turning away from her, he rose and started walking up the mountainside slowly. "I'm Teertha," she panted, scrambling up the slope behind the agile figure.

"Teertha," the man uttered the name slowly, almost as if tasting each syllable. "A beautiful name. Do you know what it means? Teertha means a pilgrim." Teertha felt a warm rush of happiness. She was no longer merely a citizen with a seven-lettered name in a ration card. On the path of life, she was (how exciting) a pilgrim.

The days seemed to fall into a strange pattern on their own. They ate berries, which sustained them for hours and sometimes when lucky, they chanced upon fresh, juicy fruit. Teertha slept in the ruins at night. "Master," she said one day. The man had said he had no name and in this strange, enchanted forest she had accepted such a fact. Anything was possible here, even nameless men.

"Master," she repeated, "I'm one confused person. My mind is like a chariot running amuck, drawn by ten horses trying to go ten different ways. Help me."

The master shook his head gravely.

"Look out for signposts and guides on the ancient highway of the mind, Teertha. No one here travels alone. Look at every face as you drive your crazed chariot. One of the thousands that you pass on your way could be a horse whisperer. Listen attentively to such a person, hold your horses with a steady hand and be ready to accept help."

There was a nip in the air. What date was it, wondered Teertha, what month? She seemed to have lost all sense of time. Luckily for her, the master never seemed to desert her for long. There he was, sauntering thoughtfully, picking up dead twigs and inspecting them closely.

"Master!" she burst out petulantly as soon as he was within earshot. "Why is it that rotters gallop to the finishing line first and nice people always finish last? Now look at that creep Nerulekar, my colleague in office – always pinching my ideas, currying favour with the boss, cutting me out of things, showing me up in a bad light...."

"You are a part of the great cosmic design, Teertha," the master's voice was stern. "Your achievements and failures are predetermined. You could oscillate a bit here and there out of course but your path has been carved out for you by a higher authority. You are a bit of the great universe, Teertha. A bubble of the infinite magic with external trimmings for identification."

"Fat lot of good being a cosmic croissant is going to do to me. Now that wretch Nerulekar...." grumbled Teertha.

"The worker gets richer for the work he does. The shirker loses a golden opportunity to evolve. Success is all about perspective, Teertha. Do not worry about the Nerulekars of the world."

Sunsets were beginning to get colourful. Pink, amethyst and saffron lit up the fluffy clouds and tinged Teertha's face with a glow at dusk. The mountainside, caught up in the mad mayhem of sundown colours turned a brilliant golden green. Teertha and the master walked to the cliff edge every evening to watch the sunsets. They could see the ruins (Teertha's sleeping chambers) far below the edge of the cliff.

"You soliloquize a lot, don't you, Teertha?" asked the master, watching her frowning distracted face.

"Oh, I spend entire days having frantic conversation with myself," answered Teertha truthfully."

"How many selves do you have?" asked the master.

"Pardon me...?" Teertha was taken aback. "Yes ... of course. I am different people at different times ..." she continued slowly.

"No, Teertha," the master's voice came soft and resonant. "All those talkative selves clamouring for attention are illusions. The quiet one, the one always in the background, listening, watching, but never passing judgement...."

"Yes, yes?" Teertha felt strangely excited.

"Ah, Teertha child, that silent self who never speaks is the real you. The silent one, the one with no ideologies or emotions ... the eternal listener, Teertha, is the real you," continued the master quietly.

Yes, thought Teertha, melting into the golden moment of the dying sun, there was no cause for distress, dichotomy or dithering.... That wonderfully solid silent watcher would always be there within her....

She felt positively friendly towards the master now. No formalities existed between them anymore and talking to him was rather like talking to herself. She could reveal her deepest insecurities to this strange nameless man.

They had stopped to watch some squirrels at play. Teertha prodded at some shrubs with her foot. She looked down all the while, embarrassed. "Master," she began tremulously, "I am attracted to this married man in my office. He is very good-looking and very talented...."

"Rainbow man!" snapped the master.

"What?" stammered Teertha.

"The mind hallucinates, Teertha, be careful. It creates someone with imaginary attributes and you fall in love with the illusion. You chase the illusion, pine for it, crave for it and when you finally come close and reach out for the object of desire...."

"Yes ... yes?" breathed Teertha.

"Your hand goes through. There never was such a person, only a mirage," said the master. "Do not squander your energies on illusions, Teertha. They are not worth it," finished the master before walking away from her.

Days were running into one another. Teertha knew she had lost weight. Her feet were full of calluses (her shoes having given way long back), her hair matted with dirt, but she felt strangely and wonderfully alive. Rarely had she felt like this back home.

"Master, I suffer from terrible depression sometimes. And

some days I feel so angsty that I can barely make it to the bus stop in the mornings. I feel that I am in danger of vanishing altogether and could do with some urgent earthing," said Teertha one day.

"Aaaah, depression," the master's voice seemed to echo along a long dark tunnel. "I know what depression is. Starker and drearier than any desert. An affliction more fatal than the cancer and more contagious than the flu." He looked up suddenly from the act of grinding something soft and white with a stone.

"Would you like to fly, Teertha?" he asked suddenly, holding up a battered white flower. "Ever had Datura?" he continued, "This is something like it. Have you ever flown?"

Teertha shook her head. The only intoxicating thing she had had in her twenty-six years of life were her father's awful homemade wines (which more often than not turned into vinegar).

"I'll have a little bit of the stuff," she said uncertainly.

"There are no half measures for flight, Teertha," said the master sternly. "Anyone who dares to fly has to be prepared to forfeit safety, sanity and comfort. When you put this white paste under your tongue, you will feel rain drumming on your brain and fire scalding your breath. Spring shall course through your veins while your chest will burst with a million strange emotions. The smell of a hundred summer flowers shall suffuse your senses while your thoughts like untamed eagles shall wing towards unknown heights. Your ears will reverberate with the beats of strange drums while a dozen unimaginable colours and horizons shall beckon you. The pleasure will stun you and the pain sear you. Are you ready?" asked the master.

"Yes," said Teertha strong-voiced, surprising even herself. "I have lived too long in a predictable prosaic world. For once in my life, I would like to fly."

When she woke up the next morning, Teertha felt as if she had travelled an entire galaxy in that one night. Never again would she ever fear anything again – the unknown, death, the Nerulekars....

Night times were beautiful. When the moon was full, Teertha walked about the hillsides with every blade of grass catching silver. The moonlight was so bright at such times that she could see the lines on her palms if she held up her hand. On no moon nights, starlight came into its own, pinpricking the entire mountainside with the sparkle of diamonds. Sometimes it rained and a certain patch of darkness came alive with fireflies. Teertha watched the mad glittering emerald dance for hours till the configuration lost strength and the fireflies dropped dead one by one, consumed by their own complex compulsive energy.

"You know," said Teertha one night, "I hate to complain all the time but I never get what I want when I want it. And by the time I get what I want, I don't seem to want it anymore."

Teertha stopped short, finding her tongue tying itself into knots.

"Ah, child, that happens to people born on the equinox," said the master.

"And I can never feel really happy, you know, deliriously

happy the way some lucky people are capable of feeling," grumbled Teertha.

"Emotions are but the temporary imbalance of the glands, Teertha. Don't go too much by them," said the master. "Do you know that there are people who feel the warmth of sunshine in the middle of a cold night and smell incense where there is none? Ah, that now is the true power of the mind. Such a mind knows no happiness and no despair but exists merely and blissfully in itself."

Would she ever be rescued, thought Teertha, whose clothes were close to falling apart. But did she want to be rescued, she wondered uneasily. Would the master go with her to the outer world (she thought of her home in that way now) if she were ever to be rescued? She missed the newspapers most of all with their headlines of death and disaster.

"Why is there so much of violence in the world?" asked Teertha with a sigh.

"Big cats eat smaller creatures; the smaller ones eat even smaller prey. And somewhere, far away, thousands of birds smash themselves against cliff sides and great white whales rise out of the sea to die in snowy silences, Teertha. Such are the laws of nature," said the master.

It was getting cooler. Was winter creeping up already, thought Teertha, walking on the woody pathways, thrashing at bushes with a branch childishly. What was that hum, was there a beehive around? The hum got louder. And then suddenly she saw it. It was a helicopter! Teertha raced to the cliff edge, ripped off her top and brandished it wildly in the air.

"Hey!" she screamed, "Hey! I'm here! I'm here!"

They had seen her and the chopper began to circle the area, dropping height all the while.

"So they've come," the voice behind her was quiet.

Teertha started guiltily.

"You'll come with me, Master? Her voice was pleading. The man shook his head. They stood facing each other silently.

"Thank you for everything, Master," Teertha's voice came out in a whisper.

"Do not ever call anyone master again, Teertha. You have only one master – yourself. The rest are mere guides. I was never your master, merely a mirror, an echo on the cliff side telling you things you wanted to hear and giving you answers that you already knew," saying which he walked slowly away.

As Teertha watched, the master seemed to get smaller with distance, his figure changing with every strip of sunlit grass between the dark brooding trees. At moments he appeared old, sometimes childlike, sometimes tall, sometimes small, sometimes solid and sometimes translucent with sunlight filtering through him.... Was he real, thought Teertha, feeling suddenly cold, or just a figment of a fevered hallucinating mind?

And then a cacophony of frantic voices seemed to envelop her. Men from the helicopter were crowding around her thrusting fresh clean-smelling clothes upon her. She was being asked to nibble on a biscuit (slowly, slowly... not too much at a time), sip distilled water ... slowly ... slowly again. She was being fussed over and cosseted as if she were a child and then gently led up the mountainside to the helicopter. They marched on, single file, four burly men and Teertha, through the thick mangled undergrowth. Teertha slowly fell back to the rear of the group almost as if reluctant to get to the helicopter. The thick-set leader of the rescue mission glanced back from time to time to make sure that she hadn't vanished, so ethereal and thin did she appear – almost capable of vanishing into thin air at any moment.

"I slept in the ruins all these nights," Teertha told the man ahead of her. He turned and stared at her strangely.

"There are no ruins here, Ma'am. They were burnt down decades back," said the man.

"But –" began Teertha and stopped abruptly. They had come to the cliff edge where Teertha and the master had stood and watched so many sunsets. Teertha stared unbelievingly. The hillock below rose gently, its virgin slopes covered with a uniform growth of short springy shrubs. There were no ruins.

She was then being hoisted into the helicopter and tucked in comfortably from all sides. A soft warm blanket was thrown around her (after all she was sure to be in a state of shock). All settled, the chopper soared into the blue sky with a deafening roar. Teertha looked down at the fast fading landscape, trying to suppress a strange tug of homesickness. "Dead Woman Returns" the newspaper headlines would scream tomorrow. "Teertha Chakravarty, air crash victim presumed dead for so many weeks, has survived miraculously..." the text would run. They would want photographs, she thought, her mind plummeting into practical mundane matters once more. The only ones she had were her passport-sized ones where she appeared slightly cross-eyed (the harrowing business of posing for close-up photographs always left her cross-eyed). A gentle cool breeze wafted into the cockpit of the helicopter.

"The mercury is dipping," the weather column would proclaim in another part of the newspaper, "and the days ahead will be cool and lovely...."

A feeling of bliss stole over Teertha. It had been a wonderful pilgrimage, all in all. She shut her eyes and slept.

THE COUNSELLOR

Piyush Ganguly stood on the ship's deck gazing out at the endless gray-blue sea. He was a long way from home. Halfway House with its dilapidated staircase and cool dark rooms seemed a galaxy away. Four months on an oil tanker was the outer limit of his threshold, he decided. After that, something within him seemed to just snap. The bleakness of the endless horizon seemed to permeate right into his bones. A cancerous kind of loneliness ate into his brain and he went around in a nervy neurotic fashion (like the other sailors on the ship) thirsting for a normal land-bound existence surrounded by warm sweating swarms of humanity.

He had five more months to go before his contract ended and he thought longingly of home. Home. Warm, sweet, comfortable home with different smells of cooking at every landing. The Guha entrance smelt the best, especially when

Khokon was home for the weekends. Fish chops and chana dal and maida luchis fried by his adoring Kakima. Lucky devil, thought Piyush grinning to himself, to have an Aunt who was devoted as well as a terrific cook!

Piyush unhooked his elbows from the railings and slowly walked back to his cabin. Evenings were the worst, he thought despondently, putting on a Grace Kelly movie for the seventh time (this ship stocked only black and white movies of the fifties). The minute sailors came back from their duties and stepped out of their boiler suits, a strange unfriendliness seemed to overtake them and they drifted away in different directions, forming little islands of isolated humanity on the vast tanker. Daytime was different. Working deep down in the ship's engine room created a kind of temporary camaraderie. The ear-splitting noise of the ship's engines, the blasting hot working conditions (which sometimes went up to 46 degrees centigrade) and the prospect of having a mammoth boiler burst in one's face kept the men bonded in a kind of fearful fellowship. But once duty hours were over and grimy gear off, the men turned strangers again ... glued mindlessly to television sets, thought Piyush sourly, or like him, draped over railings and staring out to sea with mere thoughts for company.

There was a knock on Piyush's cabin door. It was the young fifth engineer, Vasudevan. The expression on his face was harried and helpless and his body posture clearly showed that he was pregnant with some kind of disturbing news. In his hand he held an open letter.

"Yes, Vasu?" Piyush could not keep the kindliness out of

his voice even though he had a premonition about what was coming.

"It's my fiancée, Sir. Sudha. She has given me an ultimatum. If I don't get back home in a month's time, the marriage is off," Vasu's voice whittled down to a distressed squeak.

Piyush gave a small soundless inward sigh. The ever-popular Agony Aunt (or rather Uncle) facet of his personality seemed to be called for again.

' "I've tried talking to the Captain," continued Vasudevan, "but he says the company won't put me down till I complete nine months and by then it will be too late ... too late...." He wrung his hands in despair.

Piyush pulled out a sheet of white paper and pushed it across to Vasudevan. He leaned back in his seat and applied his mind to the problem in hand.

"Write!" he commanded. "'Dearest Flower-face,'"

"But she is not exactly very pretty...." protested Vasudevan unhappily.

"Write!" repeated Piyush thunderously and Vasudevan wrote. Obediently, with his head bent low, and the text of the letter unfolded itself like a flower unfurling at sunrise.

"The idea Vasu, at such times, is to write over-the-top sentimental prose that would leave you cringing at normal times. But believe me, it works wonders with women, particularly distraught unreasonable ones. What is needed at this moment is a loud vulgar declaration of love that will counteract the problems created by your delayed return home. Psychology, dear boy, is everything...."

Vasudevan walked out of the cabin, eyes shining and an expression of reverence on his face. Big boss was good!

Piyush leaned back in his seat and lit a cigarette. Women! Would they ever understand sailors, he thought wryly. What it was like to be closeted with forty other sailors on a ship (out of which one was sure to develop allergic reactions to at least a dozen)? To slog like a dog in the daytime and sleep an uneasy sleep at night, imagining fires and collisions at every little sound? To eat indifferently cooked food week after week and stare for months at the sea, seagulls and sickening faces of fellow sailors all in that order? Why, sometimes men nearly forgot what normal land life was all about. It happened to him pretty often. Every time he went home after a long voyage, Piyush stood transfixed mid-pavement, staring at everyday things like markets, potatoes and girls in minis as if they were God-given gifts from heaven. His wife Kusum had to pinch him hard to get him off the staring and shut his mouth. Women! They were so wrapped up in their own inadequacies and complexities, he thought, pursuing his pet train of thought, so fond of erecting high walls around themselves that it took husbands and boyfriends years of masonry to knock them down. His wife Kusum for example. So fond of seeing herself as a martyred heroine and perpetually whining for him to give up sea life and spend more time with her.

Kusum. Strange how he could never use with his own wife the flowery dialogues he prescribed to others. They seemed out-of-place and embarrassing somehow. He preferred to speak of happily mundane things like movies, menus and holiday plans. In his own life, the thought of discussing deeper emotions left him feeling vaguely squeamish. So they went along six years like a pair of well-oiled railway tracks, ever parallel, heading towards the same destination, but never quite destined to meet. They had their seventh anniversary coming up, Piyush suddenly remembered, and he'd better remember and make a timely phone call. A phone call from the ship was hardly a happy affair, with one's own voice ringing echoingly in the ears, but, thought Piyush, it kept egos intact, which was much more important than having a meaningful conversation.

Piyush Ganguly was not handsome. But his face invited confidences. It was an interesting face, a mixture of openness, receptivity, intelligence, good humour and an impression of vast stores of sympathy. Troubled souls gravitated towards him like flies to marmalade. His airplane journeys invariably turned into psychotherapy sessions with co-passengers, drunkards wept on his shoulders in local trains, and cadets and junior engineers thronged to his cabin in ships to unload all woes. Slowly, the realization came to Piyush that he was born to guide. To control, propel, monitor and sometimes shove people into the right path of cerebral movement. It pleased him to pen the right lines for the right occasions for people, to revive and reconstruct crumbling relationships and to play god even if it was for a few hours. Was he, a niggling worry plagued him, a control freak?

There was just one month left to go. Piyush stood on the deck (his favourite occupation) and watched the sunset, cigarette in hand. This would, most definitely, be his last voyage. He had made the decision the night before, while winding up for bed. Kusum was right. It was a lonely life for a childless woman to have a husband at sea most of the time (though his mother was very good company for his wife). It was crucial that he devote quality time to Kusum after all these years ... and yes, he'd take up a shore job for the first time in his life. He blew a ring of smoke and watched it thicken, spread and disperse into the evening air. He'd get into the regular commute-shove-sweat grind millions of people went through every day and be chained to a dreary desk job in all probability, he thought without enthusiasm.

The sea was restless. But then the South China seas invariably were. Piyush gazed at the waters mesmerized. The ocean was an ever-changing entity (so like a woman, he thought whimsically). Some days the water was calmly glassy, some days sharp and choppy, some days serene and sometimes merry with white-crested little wavelets breaking all over. And sometimes (like today) a gray and cruel lurking menace seemed to lie beneath the swell of waves. The changing colour of the sea was another thing that fascinated him. On certain days it was crystal blue, sometimes pure aquamarine and sometimes muddy brown with filthy bits of floating plastic. He had still not made that anniversary call, he remembered with a twinge of guilt, though the occasion had passed a few weeks back. But never mind, he thought, the announcement that he was giving up sea life would be the greatest anniversary gift, though maybe a little belated.

There was a low apologetic cough behind him. He turned,

quickly crushing his cigarette under his heel (this was a no-smoking zone of the ship). It was the new Nepali cadet Phu Dorje.

"Me want speak to you, Saar," said Dorje.

Piyush could guess what the problem was or rather who the problem was. Chief Officer Mishra, who believed in screaming and ranting at all newcomers and making their lives miserable from the moment they joined the ship.

"Mules, the whole lot of them. Mules!" Mishra had told Piyush once, "You have to whip them to keep them in line."

While hardened seniors had cultivated thick hides to deal with the whipping style of functioning, Dorje with his language problem and his intense homesickness for his mountain home seemed badly hit.

"Cannot take no more insult, Saar. Work like madman whole day and eat curses for dinner. First I think I jump in sea and end all. But now..." he slowly pulled out a mean looking meat knife from the folds of his trousers. "I think I kill bastard."

Whoa, this is tricky, thought Piyush in alarm. Half a dozen oil drums were lined up on the deck. He sauntered over and sat down on one, signaling Dorje to do the same.

"Sit down. And put that thing away, son. It's making me nervous," said Piyush.

Dorje obeyed sullenly and the knife vanished into the folds of his trousers once again.

"You have a wonderful name. Phu Dorje means Jupiter wisdom. Tell me, wise one, have you ever read Kahlil Gibran?" asked Piyush gazing up at the sky dreamily.

"Nu-uh. Dunno him," muttered Dorje.

"That's quite alright," said Piyush hurriedly, his tone soothing. "At your age I hadn't read him either. Do you know what the Prophet said years back?"

Piyush leaned back. Dorje looked supremely attentive, his chinky eyes nearly closed with concentration. Something profound was coming his way for sure.

"The Prophet said,

'Sons of my ancient mother, you riders of the tides,

How often have you sailed in my dreams

And now you come in my awakening, which is my deeper dream,

Ready am I to go, and my eagerness with sails full set awaits the wind.

Only another breath will I breathe in this still air, only another loving look cast backward,

And then I shall stand among you, a seafarer among seafarers,

And you, vast sea, sleeping mother,

Who alone are peace and freedom to the river and the stream,

Only another winding will this stream make, only another murmur in this glade,

And then I shall come to you, a boundless drop to a boundless ocean.'"

There was a moment's silence.

"Do you know what that means, Dorje?" asked Piyush quietly.

"Nu-uh. No understand."

"Then sit back and listen. The gist of it is that when destiny sends you to the seas for your livelihood, accept it! Accept the fog, the waves, the seagulls and a skyline that never ends. Accept the loneliness that rises out of the swirling whirlpools and scoop it into your soul. Accept the brotherhood of sailors who may never want to even look at your face but will stand by you in every storm. Accept day after day of drudgery so that you can smell flowers blooming on the mountains someday. Accept mediocre food, mindless exhaustion, illogical conduct. In short, accept Chief Officer Mishra and you shall live to see a new tomorrow!"

Piyush stopped, completely out of breath. This was quite the longest impromptu speech he had given in recent times. His pep talks, he thought in a self-depreciatory way, seemed to be steadily getting more colourful by the day.

Dorje smiled. In the fast gathering darkness it was as if a meteor had split the sky with fire. He stood up and casually tossed something at Piyush's feet where it landed with a soft clatter. It was the meat knife.

"You good man, Chief," was all he said. He sketched Piyush a crisp sailor's salute and slunk away into the darkness. Whew, breathed Piyush, he really needed that cigarette again.

Meal times were happy affairs in the ship's mess once more. The fifth engineer actually smiled over food instead of being perpetually sunk in gloom (Sudha having responded satisfactorily to the letter) and Dorje and Mishra were seen nodding civilly instead of glowering at each other across the dining hall. Piyush felt relaxed and expansive. The days were passing pretty fast (as the last ones always did) and very soon it would be time for him to be going down the gangway....

It was a cold blustery morning when Piyush signed off from the ship. The entire crew had gathered on deck to see him off.

"We'll miss you, Ganguly," the Captain said, clapping a friendly hand on his shoulder. "You were the best shrink the ship has ever had." The two men laughed. A little distance away from their superiors the junior officers waited huddled up. Piyush walked up to the group for a few last words. Dorje held out something. It was an exquisitely carved "kukri."

"For you, Chief, from my hometown Gangtok. Fond memories." He made a violent stabbing action in the air and Piyush laughed. I'll miss the blighters, he thought affectionately and started walking down to the waiting launch.

The launch set off casting plumes of dazzling white spray on either side. Piyush watched with a slight touch of nostalgia as the ship (his home for nine months) slowly diminished in size and finally became a speck on the horizon.

Tomorrow was another day. Another kind of life awaited him. He'd have to start at building up a comfortable relationship with his mother and wife again. Every time some kind of smooth equation had been arrived at in the past it had invariably been time for him to sail. This time they could all work at something that was going to be solid, linear and lasting. His mother would be delighted to hear of his decision. Her greatest wish in life was to be surrounded by famished people whom she could transport with her repertoire of awesome cooking. Piyush smiled imagining the lineup of delicacies that were sure to be awaiting him....

It was pouring with rain when the taxi stopped at Halfway House. Piyush jumped out, paid off the driver and rushed into the building like an excited schoolboy, scattering raindrops from his hair and clothes.

"Hey Khokon! I'm back! Get out that chess board," he yelled on the ground floor. Only silence greeted him. Funny, he thought, were the Guhas sleeping at this odd hour? He raced up the stairs breathlessly. Sharma Dadi was labouring down the stairs and he dived to touch her feet. She passed an abstracted hand over his head. She looked much older and more haggard, he thought.

"Hullo Dadi! How's everybody? Where's your precious Khokon? Can't seem to see him around," said Piyush breezily.

There was a strange silence.

"Khokon has passed away," said Dadi in a cold little voice. She touched a withered hand to his shoulder.

"I'm sorry, beta," was all she said before proceeding down the stairs with shaky arthritic precision.

Khokon! Dead! His head seemed to spin for a moment. He rushed up the stairs to his house on the fourth floor. The front door was open. His mother sat on a chair silently, with a vacant expression on her face. On seeing him, she seemed to rise with great effort.

"So you've come," was all she said, unsmilingly. "Here's a letter for you."

She handed him an envelope and vanished inside. He tore

the letter open. What the hell was happening? Where was Kusum? Nothing seemed to be going as per plans. The handwriting in the letter was beautifully formed, uniform and belonged to Kusum.

"Dear Piyush," it began, "I've searched and searched but can't seem to find any answers. I cannot say that our marriage is over; it didn't really start, did it?

I waited for your anniversary call, which never came. But even if it had, would a dozen clichéd words have meant anything? There is no rancour at my end and no – no other man either. It was nice while it lasted but the charade had to end. Wish you happiness always. Kusum."

A single sentence was added in the end, obviously an afterthought.

"p.s. I have been to various counsellors in these last few months but it really is no use."

THE HOSTAGE

When Subroto Dey got kidnapped on his way back home from the market, he was more surprised than frightened. It all happened with unexpected suddenness and with a very co-operative attitude being shared by both the kidnappers and the kidnapped. It was slightly disappointing at Subroto's end, no doubt, as kidnapping to his mind was supposed to be accompanied by blood, gore, thunder, lightning, bullets and action (at least that was the way it happened in the books he wrote). But what happened in real life was very quiet, dignified and vaguely anti-climaxish.

It happened like this. A woman who seemed to be going round in circles in the busy market area searching for an address, suddenly stopped the taxi, leaned out and asked him for directions. Since the directions were extremely convoluted, a request to drive a short way and point out the route had him hopping readily into the taxi and they started off with much smiles and good cheer all around.

It took Subroto a while (he always lost all sense of time in the presence of ladies) to realize that they were heading in a direction that was very different from the one planned earlier. His queries were met with smiling silence and very soon they were speeding out of city limits and onto a barren lonely motorway flanked by saltpans and herons.

And so he got kidnapped. And an ordinary Monday morning in the month of February suddenly took on a touch of the unexpected. His kidnappers couldn't have been more charming or thoughtful. The woman carried jam sandwiches, a packet of Glucose biscuits and a bottle of lemonade in a plastic bag and she offered these to Subroto at regular intervals. He declined politely. He was not ready to be drugged. Not yet. The male kidnapper (the taxi driver) put on some taped music (of the lively Shammi Kapoor variety), presumably to take the edge off the kidnapping. It was all very amicable and friendly.

Subroto Dey was forty-three, a bachelor and a writer by profession. He lived with his old mother on the fourth floor of Halfway House and wrote thrillers for a living. His own life was far from thrilling, being humdrum and dreary to the extreme. His mother cooked typically Bengali food for him day after day after day and spent time either in prayers or in watching melodramatic serials on television. The shabbily comfortable house sported mismatched pieces of furniture (inherited from ancestors over generations), faded curtains at windows and lumpy shapeless cushions. Mosquito nets were unfailingly erected over beds a little before nine, as on the dot of nine the family dramas on television commenced, rendering his mother immobile for two whole hours. The mosquito net habit had (along with the furniture pieces) been duly handed over across generations of Deys who migrated from Midnapur to Mumbai over the years. Mrs. Dey, an upright Bengali, never failed to blow the conch shell thrice at dusk and the evening aarti was accompanied by a delicious prasad of coconut shavings mixed with crumbled pedhas.

Subroto wrote his stories sitting at the dining table with an intense concentration that even the blaring television could not disturb. He often got yellow oil stains on his manuscript (the dining table was never quite wiped properly after meals) but that didn't worry him. It only added to the spice of the stories.

His stories were a revelation. They were full of fast cars, faster women, blood soaked crimes, designer labels, imported booze, awesome cigars, gangster molls, five star restaurants and expensive colognes. They throbbed with sex, violence and colour, zeroing in on life in the fast lane. Nobody in their wildest dreams could have imagined that the soft-spoken, balding "bhadralok" could write such devastating stuff. But there it was! It was as if all of Subroto's suppressed personal desires erupted into his works of fiction which in turn repaid their creator by lifting him from the quagmire of dullness and catapulting him into a glitzy make-believe world. And now that, on this lovely February morning, the action had come spilling out of the pages and into real life, he felt intrigued, excited, and ravenously hungry.

It was pitch dark when they reached a ramshackle hut on

a lonely hillside. The three of them walked gingerly in the dark, the dim light of the torch faltering alarmingly. I hope I don't die of snakebite at the very onset of my adventure, thought Subroto uneasily. On reaching the shack, the woman knocked softly thrice (so like his books). The door was opened by an elderly man who grasped Subroto's hand warmly and welcomed him in. Strange behaviour for a kidnapper, thought Subroto, not for the first time. He was given the honour of sitting on the only chair in the room. Besides the rickety chair, the room had, Subroto noticed in the light of the 40 watt bulb, an earthen matka with an upturned glass on it and a bunch of shadowy objects piled in a corner. The three kidnappers sat on the floor and looked up at him worshipfully. Once again, Subroto got the feeling that it was all unreal, maybe a dream.... The elderly man was the first to speak. His voice came out resonant and clear and, thought Subroto, much too loud to be any dream.

"We are great fans of yours, Sir and have read every single book that you've written. As for why we have got you here in this unusual fashion...."

They were petty thieves it appeared, with mastery in key duplication. They made a living from burgling houses left empty during vacations. Expertise in matters like counterfeit note-making and false passports were added qualifications. But now they felt they had evolved and wanted to move on to bigger things. What they sorely lacked was imagination and this was where he came in.

"Will you help us, Sir, with your wonderful ideas?" the taxi driver asked him imploringly.

He wouldn't get his hands dirty as all he had to do was the masterminding. And if caught, he was at liberty to say that he was drugged, tortured and threatened into being an accomplice (none of the acts would actually be implemented, they hurried to assure him). At the end of four months he would be given a hefty cut of the loot, a few bruises for authenticity and set free.

Subroto sat and thought out things. The forty-three years of his life had been gray, drab and lonely. Monotonous and monochromatic with his writing career giving him just enough to survive comfortably. And now, out of the blue, life had tossed him a googly. A fabulous opportunity to live out his stories. All his cravings could be translated into reality in one short move. What was needed was a dash of courage. The trio waited expectantly for his answer. The old man struck a match and lit a bidi. The dark objects in the corner of the room were lit up for a second and Subroto saw what they were. A country made gun, a knife and a metal rod. He hastily looked away.

"Yes," he said, smiling, "I'll go along with you."

There was jubilation in the shack. A discreet cough ensued from the old man.

"Uh-uh … a couple of men may have to be bumped off here and there…" he mumbled, trying to appear nonchalant.

There was a moment's silence.

"Oh, that's alright. After all, murder stories are my forte," replied Subroto easily.

The partnership was celebrated with toddy and stale fried fish.

Subroto settled down to business the next morning. His plans had to be put down on a roll of toilet paper as the kidnappers had forgotten about mundane things like paper and pens in their excitement. The roll of paper was pilfered from a roadside restaurant and a child's green crayon got hold of, for writing. The first event was slated to be a domestic robbery of an easy nature. An Udipi hotel owner lived with his widowed mother in a quiet colony. The mother was known to attend frequent family weddings dripping with gold. Cagey responses to doorbell summons clearly indicated a comfortable booty in the cupboards. The kidnappers had done their homework well and could furnish Subroto with all the necessary data and the operation turned out to be ridiculously simple. A bribable watchman too fond of the bottle and a New Year party to be held on the building terrace only succeeded in simplifying matters to the extreme. It was a cakewalk for the kidnappers with guests, caterers and decorators moving up and down the building all day long and a couple with a small bag was hardly noticeable. Soft gloves and skillfully chiseled skeleton keys added to the simplicity of the operation. Subroto recommended an artistic touch of slipping a single gold earring into the snoring watchman's pocket. The success of the robbery was celebrated in a slightly more sophisticated manner, with whisky and tandoori chicken being brought in for the occasion.

The second case was tricky. A middle-aged moneylender (whom the lady kidnapper owed a lot of money) had to be finished off for good. Days of tedious questioning ensued.

But the kidnappers managed to crosscheck all possible details and were able to furnish Subroto with a complete profile of Mr. A. Neotia. He travelled from Karjat to Kalyan every morning, his blood group was "A" positive, he took artificial sweeteners in his tea, and was a severe arthritic. Subroto pounced on the last bit. Yah! That was it!

Mr. Neotia got down at Kalyan at 8.57 in the morning from a fast CST-bound local and hurried off the platform along with other passengers as seven minutes later the Deccan Queen from Poona would come hurtling down the same platform sending clouds of dust and litter in all directions. Neotia, it was decided, who walked with halting arthritic difficulty, would have his briefcase and papers knocked out of his hands by a man in a hurry. Hassled, harried and bending painfully to pick up his things, he would be jostled around in the crowd, nudged, shoved and pushed inexorably towards the edge of the platform. Just as the train was thundering in, he would go over the edge and the Deccan Queen would do the rest. Four people would be better than three for this particular operation, everyone agreed, and Subroto got his first field assignment.

Subroto walked the hillside every evening at sunset. His kidnappers set him free for two hours every day. Only silhouettes were visible at this hour and it was quite safe for him to be walking around. There was no one to recognize him really as the nearest human habitation was a seldom-used stone quarry a mile away. Besides, the kidnappers had started trusting him. Trusting him to such an extent that he was well on his way to becoming the ring leader any day. The kidnappers hung on to every word that he uttered and if anything, their attitude was even more reverent than before.

Subroto sat down on a boulder and lit a home-made bidi. He had developed quite a taste for bidis of late. He found the illicitly brewed rice liquor quite exhilarating (having been a teetotaler all his life). He had changed. He knew he had. His gait was quicker, his responses sharper and a strange exuberance seemed to surge in his veins at all times. They had two murders and six thefts (all successfully executed) behind them now. A heady sense of power seemed to invade his senses. A perpetual high that story writing had never succeeded in giving him ... to plan a crime to the last meticulous detail, to supervise its execution and roam free thereafter ... was there ever a feeling so intoxicating? He got newspapers from time to time (generally as food wrappings, from roadside stalls). His kidnapping had made the headlines for a while, but now, like all sensational pieces of news, it had faded into oblivion. The papers had fresher juicier bits of news to shout out and Subroto Dey was history. He felt unbearably miffed at times to be forgotten so fast. Sometimes he had an uncontrollable urge to walk up to the nearest police station and surrender. And then stand up and shout out his crimes to the world so that it could marvel at his brains and his cunning. But good sense invariably prevailed in time and he kept silent. Three and a half months had passed since his kidnapping and he hardly had a fortnight for his contract to end. The kidnappers, he noticed, seemed to evade any discussions about the future, preferring to center conversation around the complexities of crime and criminal psychology.

Subroto opened the newspaper that he had brought to read out in the open. This was his favourite hour, browsing through the papers while the sun dipped over the horizon. It was nice to scan the spiritual column in this mesh of misdeeds. It gave him a feeling of mild penance. A small news item caught his eye.

"Gayatri Dey, mother of popular fiction writer Subroto Dey passed away in her sleep last night. She had been keeping indifferent health since her son's kidnapping three and a half month's back and succumbed to a massive cardiac arrest in the early hours of Monday morning. She was eighty-two."

The paper dropped from Subroto's nerveless fingers and blew exuberantly away into the evening wind, pages scattering in different directions. Ma was dead! His limbs seemed to give way as he collapsed onto the grass. Waves of shock, grief, regret and a deep desperation washed over him repeatedly. He lay on the grass staring blankly at the sky as eagles slowly circled far overhead. There was nothing left in his life, he thought numbly. His kidnapping had faded from public memory. The books that he wrote, he knew in his heart of hearts, were no great works of literature and unlikely to stand the test of time. Mere C-grade pulp fiction which, like their author, was immensely forgettable. He had no special friends and no close relatives whom he could turn to in lonely moments. And now, Ma was dead. She would no longer be there with her evening aarti, brandishing joss sticks and chasing him with prasad in her outstretched hand.... His mind blanked into nothingness.

When he woke up, evening stars were beginning to prick

the lavender sky and flocks of birds were winging back to their nests. He lay on the grass as memory came flooding back. He seemed unable to summon up enough energy to rise and walk back to the shack. The others would be coming back any moment. And slowly, almost with graphic precision, Subroto Dey, in his supine position, had a vision. Rather like the plots of one of his thrillers. He saw himself walking on a white beach with waves kissing his ankles. He was wearing fashionable Bermuda shorts, and an exotic woman hung onto his arm. Further back in the background, a tall glass of frothy beer stood at attention while a pair of snazzy sunglasses lay beside it catching the sun.

Slowly, almost laughably, another picture superimposed itself over the first one. A picture of the toilet pit outside the kidnappers' shack, which guarded the booty that had been collected painstakingly over the last four months and was buried deep in the ground. Which when added up would come to a very neat sum. A very neat sum indeed. Pity it had to be split four ways....

He stood up suddenly with quick fluid grace and started walking towards the shack. There was purpose in every stride. He gently opened the door of the shack on reaching, and tiptoed inside. He refrained from switching on the dim light. Instead, he walked softly to a corner of the room, bent down and rummaged around till he found what he wanted.

It was a scythe.

Pilfered from some local paddy farmer, most probably, thought Subroto wryly. His fingers closed around the handle firmly and the curved blade glittered momentarily in the light

114

of the rising moon. Yes, he thought exultantly, he would give the story an O. Henry kind of twist that he had always admired, attempted in his books but never quite succeeded in pulling off. He positioned himself behind the door and waited soundlessly. An hour later came a babble of voices and laughter. The kidnappers were coming back, most probably laden with bags of the promised dhaba dinner. This, thought Subroto, his heart hammering deafeningly, this was the moment when the chasm between fact and fiction closed forever and his life took wing. The voices came closer as the door swung open creakingly. This was the point of no return.

Subroto gathered up his strength, raised his arms and struck.

AN ELUSIVE MAGIC

Sudeshna flung down her book with suppressed violence, leaned back and yawned. She tried to be ladylike about it and yawn with her mouth shut. But boredom, lethargy and inertia had seeped into her very bones this Tuesday morning and the yawn came out open-mouthed, wide and unabashed. The tossed book lay upturned on the floor, a couple of pages bent messily under its own weight. Frenchman's Creek. Daphne Du Maurier. How apt that she should be reading such a book on this still gray morning. Didn't she feel whimsical, fey and flighty, rather like one of Du Maurier's famous heroines? Anyway, she decided, she felt nothing like what a mid-thirties housewife (with a solid banker husband and two cherubic kids) should be feeling. Ideally, her thoughts should centre around spring cleaning, low fat cooking (her husband was high on triglycerides) and the new kid-friendly methods of mental maths. But in reality she felt wild, reckless, flirtatious and just itching to throw away the shackles of decorum and do something utterly outrageous. God! If only Sister Denise from her school days could hear her favourite Head Girl's sentiments now, thought Sudeshna laughing to herself. She would be shocked beyond words and would launch into one of her preachy soprano numbers with which she invariably pulverized her erring students. Sudeshna giggled. She had wonderful memories of her convent days – her prowess as an immensely talented goalkeeper on the hockey field, her shockingly bad performances in academics throughout school and her amorous poems written for shock value and presented lovingly to the nuns. School life had been such a blast, she thought wistfully. Why did that elusive magic invariably fade away on attaining adulthood? Why did life have to become so unbearably predictable and repetitive, she thought resentfully, and each day so like the other?

Her house stretched out before her, cool, neat and lonely. Pickles was away at office, the kids at school and she had just herself for company till they all returned in the evening. I hate mid-mornings, thought Sudeshna, plumping up a cushion violently. Time seemed to come to a dead halt around this time. She switched on the television, sank into a sofa and surfed channels disinterestedly. Each channel seemed more inane than the other, she thought. One either had to watch women with blazing eyeshadow cooking and scheming in soap serials or watch songs which featured women wearing next to nothing dancing alongside men dressed for the Alps. The news channels seemed to be obsessed with a serial killer sporting an Omar Sharif moustache, who seemed to have a penchant for disemboweling pretty young victims after slitting their jugulars. Must be an ardent fan of Anthony Hopkins, thought Sudeshna sourly, switching off the television set and gazing out at the gray skies.

Okay, she thought, with a sigh, let this be a day of intense soul searching. What did she really want from life? A nebulous answer seemed to formulate itself. Excitement. Yes! Excitement was what she wanted. Excitement, magic and some out-of-this-world experience that would lift her from her well-oiled life with its trappings of complacency and send her on a roller coaster ride. She loved her husband Pickles to distraction, with his forty-six inch waistline and his wonderful sense of the comic, but she wouldn't mind some lean, mean and hungry stranger walking into her life – a Rhett Butler-like touch after the chronic comedy of a Johnny Lever. Nothing deep, nothing disturbing, nothing that would rock the boat of blissful domesticity. Just a touch of temporary magic....

Her nails needed painting. There was a parent-teacher meeting at school the next day (a monthly highlight in her well organized life) and she'd better get groomed for the event. She rose purposefully and started rummaging through her cosmetics.

The parent-teacher meeting droned on for over an hour. The teacher, a grim-faced battle-axe, seemed determined to send the gathered parents on a guilt trip. The students' spellings were pathetic, they were informed, their grammar atrocious, their behaviour wild, and their lunch box contents shocking. At this point she glared at the parents, reducing them to quavering masses of jelly. Fast food, no doubt very convenient and quick, never did great things for children. Mothers, she said caustically, would be better advised to get up a little early and pack solid food for the children. Suitably chastised, all the mothers bent their heads and stared at their toes.

Sudeshna, nearly nodding with sleep and boredom, realized that her left foot was numb and nearly senseless. She gave it a sharp jerk to wake it up and smartly kicked the man sitting in front of her.

"Oh, I'm so sorry," she breathed out in soft apology.

The man turned and smiled at her. Gosh, she thought, going breathless, he could have come out of the movies. Who is this gorgeous hunk, she thought interestedly, haven't ever seen him before. But the students' examination answer papers were being brought in for scrutiny and all thoughts of handsome hunks fled from Sudeshna's mind. She pored over her sons' papers. They have both done well, she thought with satisfaction, and could be happily treated to the promised Spiderman movie over the weekend. A pizza dinner could also be thrown in as an added incentive to do better next time.

Sudeshna walked out of the cool dim interiors of the school and onto the road. She would have to take a taxi back home to Halfway House and not a single one was in sight as she stood in the blazing October sun. A long gleaming car drew up and stopped before her.

"Lift, Ma'am?" said an unknown voice. Sudeshna blinked at the driver, her vision blurred by the sun in her eyes. Recognition came a second later. It was Mr. Tall-dark-kind-of-handsome whom she had kicked in true Beckham style some time back in class.

"Thanks," said Sudeshna, sliding into the passenger seat even before she realized what she was doing. The man gave a low laugh as he started the car and they moved off into the still, sun-baked afternoon. There was a strange combination of smells in the interior of the car. Expensive cologne, excitement and an indefinable something else. What was the word she was looking for, she thought searching her memory. Yah, "pheromones," wasn't it? She had a split second's urge to ask him to stop the car, get down and walk away. But the moment passed. She leaned back into the seat and made herself comfortable. Blow common sense, blow middle-aged morals and seize the day, she told herself bracingly.

"Are you a parent?" she turned to ask him.

"No. A relative," he answered.

"Whose?"

A traffic cop's angry whistle drowned out his answer as the car sped past a red light. Sudeshna glanced back to see the cop waving angrily at them to stop, but the car just picked up speed.

"Nice escape. Should we celebrate that?" his voice seemed to hold a laugh.

The car swung into a cosy-looking hotel. They got down and the man ordered beer. What am I doing, thought Sudeshna in amazement, gazing at the gold and froth of her beer. Guzzling beer in the company of an utter stranger in a strange hotel? Was she feeling alright in the head? And what if some familiar person were to see her and report to Pickles? Oh, blast appearances, blast safety and security, she thought rebelliously. Excitement had come knocking at her door and she was going to live life to the hilt. At least for today. Suddenly, it felt nice to worry whether her hair was in place or not after having thought snack boxes, sock crises and dinner menus for aeons.

"Do you have change? I have just notes of five hundreds," said the man.

Sudeshna groped around in her bag, paid off the waiter and then they were on the road again, speeding into the evening. They were leaving familiar landmarks behind and seemed to be heading for the outskirts of the city. A heady kind of intoxication was upon her, partly due to the beer and partly due to the man at her side, thought Sudeshna woozily. She sprang out of her reverie as the car grated harshly over a speed breaker. They were passing a lake choked with water hyacinth. Surely not Powai Lake, she thought in disbelief. They were a long way from home and heading further away with every passing minute. She didn't have too much money in her purse either, she suddenly realized. Sudeshna felt her first twinge of alarm. The sun, she realized with a jolt, was disturbingly low over the horizon.

"I really should be getting back," she said, sitting up straight and keeping her voice firm and pleasant.

The man laughed, a charming sound, and picked up speed. Sudeshna quelled a momentary surge of panic.

"I insist we turn back now," she said in a louder tone, trying to keep her voice from shaking.

The man turned and looked at her for a second, threw his head back and laughed long and hard again. Only this time the laugh was not charming. It was strange, hysterical and did not seem to stop. Sudeshna stared at him with horrified fascination. His eyes glinted in an over bright, glittery manner. His face seemed to be catching strange and familiar shadows in the red light of the setting sun.

Recognition hit her like a dash of icy water. That Omar Sharif moustache, those rugged features, the lineup of six gruesome murders and the Hannibal style of operating.... She sat cold and motionless, unable to even croak out for help. Her flesh was crawling with fright. What had Sister Denise said years back in the Moral Science class ... "Think twice before you wish for something, girls, as your wish might just be granted." Sister Denise. Singing hymns at assembly time, bathed in morning sunlight. Was there anything so beautiful and normal, she thought, hot tears stinging her eyes. Why, why, oh why, she thought in despair, had she traded time-tested codes of behaviour for a moment of madness? The speedometer showed seventy. There was a resounding crash and then darkness.

Sudeshna woke up to find herself lying on the wooden bench of a small suburban police station. A constable was trying hard to revive her with chilled Coca Cola and there seemed to be a lot of commotion going on in the adjoining room. The constable seemed to be under the impression that splashing the victim with Coke was as effective as making her drink it and Sudeshna awoke to find her face awash with droplets of Coke.

"Madam! You are conscious," the elderly constable breathed out a sigh of relief.

"The driver is dead. Wanted for six murders," added the constable with ill-concealed relish. His expression then sobered.

"You would have been the seventh one, Madam, had it not been for the car accident," his tone was low and serious.

And suddenly Pickles was bustling into the tiny police station looking frazzled and perplexed. Wondering, no doubt, thought Sudeshna guiltily, why he had been summoned and what his wife was doing in this far-flung police station looking frightened and disheveled. She swung herself off the bench and ran to him and hugged him tight. He smelt of tobacco, antacid and prawn curry. She inhaled the amalgam of smells ecstatically, with her eyes shut. Was there ever such a wonderfully sane combination of smells, she wondered happily. She suddenly felt as if she was coming home after a long journey.

The drive home was full of a questioning silence from Pickles' end. She had a lot of explaining to do, she knew. But she had a deep comfortable conviction that Pickles would understand. Understand that elusive magic that made the most predictable people stray at times. Understand the occasional naughty wind that blew across people and made them behave in a way that was totally out of character. Such things did not occur in his bookkeeping or profit and loss accounts at work. But Pickles would understand. Period.

She turned and looked at him carefully for the first time in months. There was a touch of gray at his temples and worry lines ran down the sides of his mouth. His shirt ends parted company between buttons due to the swell of his paunch and Sudeshna felt a rush of affection welling up within her.

The children would have turned the kitchen upside down in her absence, she was sure, and would be waiting to surprise her with a tray full of rock hard cookies learned from a television program. She'd choke over a couple smilingly and discreetly feed the rest to the dog tomorrow. Tomorrow was another day. To wake up and absorb life with all its small beautiful moments.

"I'll dye your hair tomorrow," she told Pickles.

He turned from his driving and smiled. Tomorrow, thought Sudeshna with happy optimism, was sure to be lovely.

THE PICNIC

It had been a yearly practice to have a winter picnic for the residents of Halfway House. Winter was the time when monsoon grass grew tall and brown, when there was a comfortable nip in the air and spirits (with the Christmas holidays looming large and close) were always a little high and tipsy. The practice came to an abrupt halt after Khokon's suicide and an uneasy truce seemed to hang between the residents since then.

But, thought Santanu Ray, who lived on the third floor and was considered the in-house visionary, life goes on even if a couple of fellow players fall out of the race, and it was high time the annual event was revived. Santanu belonged to that near-extinct category of people who continued to uphold the concept of universal brotherhood in the face of the worst adversity. With a warm magnanimous nature that embraced all life forms, from sweepers to stray dogs and from cockroaches to clowns, Santanu deeply believed in the innate goodness of mankind as a whole. Antisocial behaviour, he was fond of telling people, was nothing more than an unfortunate quirk in life's circumstances and an accidental detour in one's genetic journey. No one could really be blamed for such things, he emphatically declared, and nursed a vast sympathy for criminals and crime at all times. He happily attained the age of fifty-eight, continuing to believe that the milk of human goodness flowed in every vein and it was this blinkered wishful thinking that made him take the initiative in the matter of the winter picnic.

Santanu went around like a man demented in the first fortnight of December. A van or a bus would have to be organized, food, drinks, games, mats, insect repellants, cushions for the ladies (particularly the asthmatic Bubla)…. He went around in a frenzy of activity, enjoying himself hugely. Why, he thought with pleasurable anticipation, it was almost as exciting as the Durga Puja preparations that started months in advance….

It was a cool crisp morning when the twenty-five members strong picnic party started out at the crack of dawn. The air was sharp and cutting. Windows of the bus were quickly rolled up as the passengers huddled into their shawls and jackets. They were to stop just once for hot roadside tea and then proceed to Lonavala, two hours from Mumbai. Conversation within the bus was limited and of a stilted kind. It was the first time in three years that they were all together like this and a feeling of resentful self-consciousness seemed to hang in the air. When the bus finally drew into its destination, the passengers stepped out into the cool mountain air with visible relief.

Afternoon spilled golden and quiet over the picnic party. Lunch was over. Lunch had been an eclectic mixture of fares. Typically Bengali food for the orthodox Bongs (the Guhas and the Boses), Punjabi fare for the "balle balle" lot (the Sharmas and their visiting cousins), salads and low calorie items for the young ladies, and a variety of pastries for the children. Santanu Ray, in a wild attempt to update his image from "middle-aged fuddy-duddy" to "upbeat and hip-hop-happening" had brought in a dash of Thai, Mexican and Lebanese flavours, which proved to be wildly popular. Yes! Lunch, thought Santanu with smug satisfaction, had been a rocking success.

Adults lay sprawled around on the hillside chatting and playing bridge. Action-packed games were done with before lunch and badminton rackets, shuttlecocks and balls lay in happy abandon on the grass. A little distance away, thirteen-year-old Milli Ray moved soft footed amidst the tall grass, swooping down with quiet cunning on unsuspecting little butterflies and imprisoning them in a glass jar for her nature study class. Further away, Pulok Sinha, sixteen, ambled around aimlessly trying to capture the forest magic on his newly gifted Nikon camera. Time stretched out uninterrupted on the mountainside and there was an idyllic picture-book quality to the picnic scene.

Malaika won the first round of bridge (as she always did). Supriya, who considered herself the better player sat up affronted. She could have won hands down, she told the others coldly, if the game had been played properly at a table. But lying twisted in the grass with caterpillars sneaking up one's ankles was hardly conducive to good bridge playing. Siddharth Sinha, her bridge partner laughed good-naturedly, shuffling the cards in readiness for the next game. He looked up once in a while to check out on his two sons Partho and Pulok.

Sharma Dadi flung down her cards after the next game and rose with stiff-limbed difficulty. She stretched creakingly and gazed around at the wooded scenery.

"I'll have a walk before I go stiff as a corpse," she laughed, beginning to hobble away.

"I'll come with you," said Rekha Guha, tossing aside her cards and rising quickly. She had been very quiet the whole morning and her eyes shone with unshed tears. The two women moved away, strolling towards a copse of trees on the hillside.

"I miss Khokon," whispered Rekha Guha in a soft shaky voice.

Sharma Dadi shot her a sharp glance.

"We all miss him. He was as much our son as yours, Rekha" she said quietly.

"But you are just a neighbour. I was the biological mother. The umbilical cord never snaps, even in death...." Rekha Guha burst into tears.

"And did you think of that when you pushed Khokon into that blasted medical college?" Sharma Dadi turned on her white-faced.

"What do you mean? Are you trying to say that I am responsible for my son's death?" bit out Rekha Guha furiously.

The two women faced each other like boxers in a ring, their bodies tense and taut.

"Did you ever bother to understand your son? His dreams, his aspirations (or rather lack of them), his childlike nature? Why, your sister-in-law understood him much better than you, his mother, ever did," the words tumbled out cruel and frank.

"You horrible old woman, you and my sister-in-law have always ganged up against me, painted me the villainess of the piece, pampered Khokon, distorted his vision..." Rekha Guha's voice rose shrilly.

A flock of wood pigeons flew out of the treetops in alarm. It was a no-holds-barred fight.

"The tragedy could easily have been averted if the right people had shown some common sense at the right time. You think I don't miss him? I loved him as much as I would my own son..." Sharma Dadi's voice grated out harsh and high.

Dark clouds were gathering at the horizon, suffusing the forest with an eerie kind of light. A restless wind seemed to spring out of nowhere....

On the other side of the hillock, Mithu Sengupta sat on a boulder with dainty grace, checking her nails for chipped nail polish. There was nothing she hated more than chipped nails, crumpled clothes and unkempt hair. Mithu led a linear uncomplicated life where the only things that mattered were the latest shades in lipsticks, the trendiest shops in town and the grooviest guys on the block. Possessing such a wonderful, one-track, focused mind gave her a look of perpetual serenity and she was a smash hit with the boys. Partho Sinha could be seen revolving around her at a radius of three feet, looking rather like an infatuated puppy.

Teertha watched the entire scene with undisguised disgust. That flirtatious minx Mithu! Always trying to be the femme fatale and hook the guys around, she thought viciously. And trying to upstage Bubladi who sat a little way off looking thin, forlorn and lonely. Poor Bubladi, with her gray asthmatic skin tone, her antiseptic spinsterish air, who never really stood a chance with men. Teertha stood up with sudden resolution, looking rather like an angry little tigress. She adored her Bubladi and it was time, she felt, to do some skilful politicking on her behalf (something she was very good at), and also put that fake beauty queen in her place. She had a sudden urge to box Partho Sinha's ears. Why couldn't he see Bubladi for what she was — a woman with the most wonderful of qualities? Instead, he continued to look at her with that stupid male myopic vision! Bubladi and Partho would make a wonderful couple, she thought happily walking towards them, and Bubladi, she suspected, always had a soft corner for Partho....

"Hey everybody! There's a touch-me-not bush here," nature lover Milli Ray's excited voice floated across the meadow and a dozen people clambered up and rushed to prod at the shy creepers and watch their leaves buckle up.

Mr. Shashank Bose and Mr. Alok Sengupta were left sitting on the grass, enmeshed in an uneasy silence. Mr. Bose pulled out a pack of cigarettes and offered it to Mr. Sengupta.

"I'll be coming over to your place to collect the Durga Puja donation," he said in an attempt at conversation. Shashank Bose was a prominent member of the local Puja Association.

"I'm afraid I won't be able to shell out much this year. I've just wrapped up some major construction work in my house," said Alok coldly. "Whose costs," he added in a nasty tone, "were supposed to be split up two ways."

There was a moment of silence.

"Well, I had offered to pay for half the bathroom water-proofing. But it should have been done at my convenience. Can you imagine the din the workers made just when Bubla had her M.A finals? She could barely study!" said Shashank angrily.

"Yes, yes ... even my Partho had problems studying through the din," Siddharth Sinha who had drifted in added his two penny worth.

"You should have done the work at a convenient time," declared Shashank.

"And what, may I ask, is a 'convenient time' according to you? It seems to come once in a light year," said Alok in a tone of growing anger.

"Well, if you had a marriageable daughter, you would understand what leakage meant. The waterproofing should have been done years back. Why, the only time a prospective groom seemed to like Bubla, he got a cupful of sewage water, thanks to your rotten loo upstairs. But you wouldn't know that, would you? Your daughter is such a flirt, you won't have to bother about arranged marriages," spat out Shashank viciously.

131

Alok Sengupta shot to his feet, towering over the still sitting Shashank, his hands balled into fists. He seemed to be holding himself in check with great effort.

"Here! Here! Easy, easy, easy ... no harsh words today," Siddharth Sinha flapped around, trying to pacify the two men. Lightning flashed somewhere, lighting up the scene in silver for a second. Thunder rumbled distantly, a minute later. Strange forces seemed to be at play in the forest and the carefree quality of the picnic seemed to be vanishing fast with the daylight. There was a feeling of evil, of impending disaster....

A piercing scream sliced the evening. Shashank Bose sprang to his feet.

"That sounded like Pulok," he said, beginning to run. The picnickers were coming running from all directions, heading for the cliff edge by some common unspoken consent. Pulok had last been seen sauntering around the cliff edge trying to capture the sunset spectacle on his camera.

"Oh, my god. He's fallen off," groaned Shashank Guha leaning over the edge.

Pulok lay on a precariously situated narrow ledge about fifteen feet below the cliff edge. His eyes were closed and he seemed unconscious. Below him stretched the ravines, terrifyingly and cruelly deep. The narrow ledge, unequipped to take human weight seemed to be giving way softly. A babble of hysterical voices rose from the gathered group.

Bubla felt her memory jolted by some invisible force. She seemed to remember something hazily. Yes! A filthy tattered rope on the path to the picnic spot. She raced away, asthma

132

forgotten in the panic of the moment and was back with the rope seconds later.

"Good girl," Partho said approvingly.

"Secure it to the boulder," snapped Shashank Bose, while the others hurried to obey his orders.

The boulder is not big enough. God, don't let there be another death, thought Rekha Guha wretchedly. She grasped the rope with her bare hands to give it some additional support.

"Here, let me..." said Sharma Dadi, grasping the rope alongside Rekha Guha.

"You shouldn't at your age, Mrs. Sharma," said Rekha Guha worriedly.

"Oh, come off it Rekha, I'm not all that much older than you. If you can do it, so can I," declared Sharma Dadi.

The two women held on to the rope tightly, bonded for a moment by imminent danger, all previous animosity forgotten....

"I'm going down," said Shashank Bose, tying the other end of the rope around his waist, "Give me a hand."

Alok Sengupta held Shashank's hand in a grip of steel as he went over the edge. For a second, Alok's broad back shut out all the others from view. Their eyes met. One small push, unnoticed by the others, the slightest of shoves from Alok would send Shashank, Pulok and the ledge crashing into the ravine below. And nobody would be wiser. All the seething resentment piled up over the years, all the unsolved issues would be wiped clean in one swift move.

"Be careful," was all Alok said in a quiet voice, as Shashank started his descent.

It was touch and go. Gathering up the injured and now wide awake and whimpering Pulok, hoisting him piggy back and groping up the cliff side while everybody pulled at the rope. They staggered to the top just as the ledge, a refuge for some vital moments, took a final curtain call and crumbled into nothingness below.

They lay around on the grass, gasping, panting and gathering their wits together. Pulok seemed to have nothing more than a twisted ankle and was more frightened than hurt. He sat moaning softly while his parents hugged him tight. The girls got up and slowly started gathering up the picnic things and stuffing them into baskets. The picnic party rose tiredly and trudged back to the bus supporting the limping Pulok between them. The hillside, so picturesque in the morning, seemed to have taken on a sinister hue and the group seemed eager to get away from it all. Back to Mumbai, thought Bubla longingly, back to crowds, lights, noise, safety....

The drive back home was full of a pregnant kind of silence. Nobody was in a mood for speech. Every mind seemed wrapped up in private thoughts, yet a warm connectivity ran through the passengers in the bus. We'll never forget this picnic, thought Santanu Ray, running a shaky hand through his thinning hair. All twenty-five of us will remember this picnic for life.

But there had been a twenty-sixth person at the picnic.

A person who had given ample signals of approaching disaster and propelled people to quick and correct actions. A person who had made sure that the ledge held till help arrived.

Who had brought years of simmering grievances out into the open and cleared the air for good. A person who had made sure that the camaraderie and bonhomie that existed at Halfway House came right back where it belonged....

Khokon Guha had been present at the picnic, as they all knew. A tangible presence, felt and sensed by each person at some time during the day. Khokon, thought Santanu Ray fondly, warm, caring, wonderful Khokon. Ever thoughtful, ever helpful. Genetically programmed, he thought with affection, falling back on his favourite terminology, to do good to his fellow beings at all times.

In life and in death.

Kankana Basu is a commercial artist by profession and has worked as an illustrator and visualizer for various advertising agencies. All along she has been moonlighting as a freelance writer for various publications, writing short stories, essays and humour pieces on a wide range of subjects – from current affairs to psychology, fashion and interior decoration. She is currently a regular freelancer for several newspaper supplements. From time to time, she also assists in the translation of stories written by her grandfather, Saradindu Bandopadhyay. She is married to a marine engineer, and has two sons aged thirteen and eleven. Most of her stories were written while sailing on the high seas with her husband.